I0525720

# The Heart of Ruth

# johanna pascall

Ark House Press
PO Box 1722, Port Orchard, WA 98366 USA
PO Box 1321, Mona Vale NSW 1660 Australia
PO Box 318 334, West Harbour, Auckland 0661 New Zealand
arkhousepress.com

© Johanna Pascall 2020

This is a work of fiction. Names, characters, businesses, places, events, locales, and incidents are either the products of the author's imagination or used in a fictitious manner. Any resemblance to actual persons, living or dead, or actual events is purely coincidental.

Cataloguing in Publication Data:
Title: The Heart of Ruth
ISBN: 978-0-6487607-2-6 (pbk)
Subjects: Fiction; Religion;

Design by initiateagency.com

To Joe, Susie and Phoebe
— we've a team

# CHAPTER 1

*W*hen your life is one big dance party, you're never really prepared for the day when the music is cut off and the dancing stops. So, when that day came for me, I certainly wasn't expecting it. And I was definitely not prepared for it.

It all started innocuous enough. I woke up with a throbbing head and parched throat - classic signs of a hangover. Signs I knew all too well having woken up in this condition every weekend for as long as I could remember and every single day for the past month as we travelled across Europe. We were following the summer music festivals and the month was a blur of alcohol and dance parties. Oh what a way to celebrate the end of school! In a couple of months we were all off to university and so we were determined to make the most of our summer break.

An intrusive ringing reverberated in my head and I realised that the noise was the reason I woke up in the first place. It was coming from the hotel phone and I could tell by the way it was ringing in my ear that I was probably the closest to it. I sighed and let it ring, hoping whoever was on the other end would give up or by some miracle, my boyfriend Kane, who's soft snore I could hear next to me, would wake up and pick up the phone. A couple of minutes passed and neither scenario happened.

Instead, the phone rang incessantly, exacerbating the pounding in my head.

With a sigh, I forced myself to open my eyes and I lifted my head ever so slightly. Next to me, Kane continued to sleep. Man, he was gorgeous. Dark hair, blue eyes and those muscles! He was a working model thanks to good genes and good connections. His Dad was a legendary rock star and his mother was an A-list Hollywood actress in possession of five BAFTAs, several Oscars and numerous other awards. He could have had his pick of a catwalk of models, yet unbelievably, he chose me. Oh, I knew I was considered "beautiful" but I wasn't without flaw, unlike the models he associated with.

Across the Shangri-La Paris penthouse suite, my best friend Eve was passed out, her platinum blonde hair was splayed across her face and next to her was the cute French boy she took back to our suite the night before and who had also woken up and at that very moment was groaning while he nursed his head in his hands.

"Please shut the hell up." My voice cracked. He didn't even bother acknowledging me but thankfully he stopped making that awful noise. The phone rang again after a short pause and begrudgingly, I reached out and answered, "Hullo?"

"Mademoiselle Ruth Triggs?" The voice on the other line was friendly. His French accent was thick but clear.

"Yup, that's me. This better be important." I muttered impatiently.

"Oui mademoiselle. This is Pierre from the reception desk. Your mother is on the other line asking to be connected most urgently. She says it's an emergency. May I put her through?"

My mother? Emergency? The sense of foreboding immediately washed away any fogginess in my head. I was instantly awake. I sat up.

Something was up. And it couldn't be good. My voice trembled as I answered, "Yes."

It was only a short pause before I heard my mum, "Ruth, I've been calling your mobile…" Her voice was quiet and it sounded hoarse. I could tell she'd been crying. A daughter could pick up these subtleties, even over the phone.

"Mum, what's wrong?" I couldn't concentrate on anything except for the wild beating inside my chest. I braced myself for the answer.

But Mum didn't answer. Instead, I heard her breathing. Heavy, strained breaths. Then I heard her sobbing.

"Mum? Tell me what's wrong? What's happened?" By this stage, Eve had also woken up and she could hear the obvious distress in my voice. Wearing only a white t-shirt, she knelt down in front of me and she whispered, "What's going on, babe?"

Beside me, Kane stirred but didn't wake.

Finally I heard a voice on the line, but it wasn't Mum's, it was my older sister Olivia. "Ruth… I'm sorry but you need to come home…" Her voice was only a whisper at the start but then she too started to sob and she made a strange noise, almost like a high shriek. Yet even before she continued, I already knew what was coming. Somehow, I just knew. Because there could only be one thing that could bring both my mum and my sister this much distress - this much pain. My heart stopped and then it was as if I could feel it literally break into pieces so I held my free hand to my heart as I felt the ache deep in my chest. I felt streams of tears running down my cheeks and I watched them fall like big fat blobs down from my jaw to my lap. Finally, Olivia broke the news, "It's Dad and the boys. There's been an accident. They're gone Ruthy! They're dead."

Three hours later, I found myself sitting in Eve's father's private jet as we made our way back to London. Kane sat next to me. Eve and the rest of our group decided that they were going to continue their holiday, but she did kindly organise for their private jet to take me home. I wasn't surprised that my so-called best friend wasn't by my side right now. Eve liked drama, but only if she was the protagonist. She didn't like being casted as a supporting actress so of course she bowed out. I should be mad at her but frankly I didn't care because right now I was living a nightmare that I wished I could wake up from. My father and two brothers were gone. Forever. Tears continued to fall. It hadn't stopped staining my face since Olivia gave me the news that morning. My eyes were swollen, they ached but I couldn't stop the tears. Any external pain was nothing compared to the pain that was in my heart.

My father was the sweetest dad. He was the most amazing father anyone could hope for. His whole life revolved around his family - around us. He was always there at our dance and music recitals, football games and school assemblies. He and Mum never missed a single event. He took the time to take Olivia and I on weekend shopping sprees to Paris, Milan, New York and he took the boys on their adventures. They did that every year without fail. Last year, Dad and the boys went trekking through Iceland. The year before that they went sailing in the South Pacific. This year was going to be their best one yet - hiking to Machu Picchu. But they never made it. While driving to Cusco, a bus driven by a drunk driver ploughed into their car. A head-on collision. Olivia said they would have died instantly. Even in a four-wheel drive, they never stood a chance.

Kane touched my arm and whispered, "We're descending."

The flight from Paris to London took less than an hour. Soon, Kane was leading me through the private terminals in Farnborough Airport.

Outside I spotted our driver, Jeb. He'd been with the family a long time. I could see that he'd been crying too but he didn't say a thing. He merely nodded in acknowledgement, opened the rear door to our white AMG sedan and took my luggage from Kane.

I hopped in and was surprised that Kane didn't follow. Instead he bent down, kissed me on the cheek and said, "I'll come by soon. I'll head home and freshen up." He didn't bother waiting for a response. He banged the door shut and I watched as he walked away.

So there I was, at the back of the car, alone with my torturous thoughts for the hour-long drive back home.

More tears flooded my eyes as I recalled the drive to this very airport a month ago. Dad insisted on dropping me off despite my firm protests that I was seventeen and therefore didn't need my parents to see me off. I was embarrassed but not because they treated me like a child, but because it was obvious that I came from a happy home. My mum and dad were ridiculously happy together and absolutely adored and spoiled their four children. I didn't like to flaunt our "happy family" to my friends who were constantly complaining about their dysfunctional families. Especially Eve. Her father was an absolute 'expert' in marriage seeing how he was now up to his fifth and his latest wife was only two years older than Eve and I. Mr. St. John was a classic case of Peter Pan Syndrome, hence the young wives, expensive toys and the lack of any paternal attention to his own children.

He was the antithesis to my own Dad who wanted to be involved in our lives. He liked being around us. My last memory of him was me kissing him on the cheek and then telling him firmly to stay in the car. I wish I had let him go into the airport like he wanted to. I wish I had let him hug me tightly the way I knew he wanted to. If I had known it was going to be the last time –

And it dawned on me… there was no "happy family" anymore. That was all gone. Dad was gone. Kyle, my big brother was gone. And Mark who was only ten years old, he was gone too! Half of my family was wiped out. Just like that. A loud sob escaped from deep within me. Once one escaped, more followed. I was alone in the back seat, crying uncontrollably, wailing even, and I was calling out for Dad, for Kyle, for Mark. I'd kept some level of composure in front of Kane and my friends, but now, while all alone in the backseat, I couldn't help but fall apart.

Meanwhile, Jeb kept driving but when I peered through the curtain of my tears at the rear-view mirror, I could see him crying as well. This made me cry even louder.

Later, I noticed that we were finally entering south London. My Dad, Eli Triggs was an infamous investor. Thanks to his Midas touch we lived in one of Belgravia's upscale streets in an opulent townhouse once owned by the Duke of Sandringham. Every investment my dad touched was a resounding success and, with the additional perk of being the younger brother of a Baron, doors always opened when my Dad knocked. And so we lived like any of those considered 'the elite' – private schools, designer clothes and a bevy of servants who waited on us hand and foot.

As soon as the car stopped in front of our home, I jumped out and ran up to the door. Harrison, our butler, was already holding the door open. Olivia stepped into view on top of the white marble staircase. Her blonde hair was a mess, in fact she looked like a mess. We ran into each other's arms and we both collapsed in the middle of the stairs, crying and holding each other. My head rested on Olivia's right shoulder, my tears stained her red silk top and I could feel her every shake, every ragged breath. I couldn't say how long we stayed like that. But it felt good to be hugged, to cry together. It was just Olivia and I now. Oh how we used to complain and moan about the boys. About the stupid tricks Kyle used to play on his little sisters like the spiders left on our pillows and the shaving cream spread all over our faces while we slept. Years later, when Mark was born, we complained about how he took up all our parents' attention or how annoying he was because he followed us everywhere, even to the bathroom! I sobbed and hugged Olivia even tighter as a multitude of memories played in my mind. I knew then that life would never ever be the same again.

# CHAPTER 2

hree days later, dressed in designer black from head to toe, I sat in Worcester Cathedral staring at the three white wooden caskets in front of me. The white roses that blanketed the caskets were beautifully arranged and they were made even more ethereal as they were gently touched by the sunlight that filtered through the stained-glass windows. It was as if God himself was beckoning Dad, Kyle and Mark, home.

Staring back at me were their smiling faces. Their large framed photos were standing beside each casket, I guess so we knew which was which. Not that you could mistake which one was Mark. His casket was notably smaller, drawing attention to the fact that a child laid there.

Mum sat to my right and she was sobbing. I could see in the corner of my eye that Olivia's hand was holding my mum's. Uncle Mo, aka Baron Moseley, Dad's older and one and only sibling, was saying something in front of the packed cathedral but the words were not registering in my head. My mind was mash and at this point I felt nothing. It was like I'd flicked the "off button" to my emotions. However, because tears were absent from my eyes, I felt guilty, I should be crying so that everyone knew that I was mourning for my dad and for my brothers. After all, they were worth mourning for. They were amazing people. But the last tears I shed were those with Olivia on the day I came home. After that I pulled myself together, especially after seeing just how paralysed my mum was with grief. She wasn't eating, she wasn't talking and instead she spent the last few days in bed. Olivia and I had been looking after her. I knew I had to be strong for my mum so I hadn't allowed myself to feel. To cry. To be angry. To mourn. To want to lock myself away from the world the way Mum had.

Meanwhile, Uncle Mo made all the arrangements for the funeral. He also made the decision that Dad and the boys were going to be buried in the family plot in his estate just outside Worcester. I wasn't sure whether he even bothered to consult my mum. Everyone knew he didn't like her very much. Even I knew that he disapproved of her because she wasn't from the "right family". My maternal grandparents had passed now but they were just normal folks - an office worker and a primary school teacher, before their retirement. I never really knew them despite the fact that they also lived in London. I suspected that Mum tried to forget her past so she could fit into Dad's world. I did see her crying one day when I was about ten years old and she said it was because her Dad died of a heart attack and a few years later I heard that her Mum died of cancer.

Uncle Mo finally finished speaking and he stepped down from the pulpit. He was a tall, skinny man with balding head and a straight nose. He looked just like Dad, except his expression was always stern, always cold, so unlike Dad who was always smiling, always laughing.

I found myself thinking back to three years ago when Olivia and I stumbled home drunk at three a.m., laughing and making quite a ruckus. Mum was waiting for us and she was absolutely livid. Dad, on the other hand was in hysterics as he watched us trying to hold each other up. Mum wanted us punished but Dad argued that we would grow out of it like he did. They argued about us constantly and this particular argument lasted for days.

Kane took my hand, signaling that the funeral service was finished. It was time to head back to the estate. Olivia helped Mum up and I dropped Kane's hand to also assist my mum who was struggling to get up. She leaned on Olivia and I as we walked down the cathedral aisle and I could feel everyone's eyes on us. I could feel everyone's sympathy. I took a deep breath and kept my eyes down, watching my black Louboutin-clad feet take one step after the next until we were inside our sedan. Mum sat between Olivia and I and Kane took the front seat next to Jeb. Soon we were following the hearses and all I could hear was Mum's non-stop agony-induced wailing.

The wailing continued but it was louder because this time it came from both Mum and Olivia as Dad, Kyle and Mark were lowered one by one into the ground. The finality of that moment hit me in the gut and I struggled to breathe. This was the last time I would be this close to Dad and the boys. Once their bodies were buried, it really was all over. I would never see them again. My chest tightened even more and a lone tear escaped from my left eye. I wiped it away.

Tomorrow, we would go back to London. Tomorrow, we would be expected to carry on. Without Dad. And without the boys. Oh how I wished I didn't have to face tomorrow.

Early the next day, I found myself sitting in Uncle Mo's office. He was lounging on a large leather chair at his antique desk and opposite him sat Mum, Olivia and I. Mum looked even thinner and paler than she did yesterday. Olivia, on the other hand, looked spectacular in her black leather pants and designer black singlet. In my jeans and t-shirt, I knew I was under-dressed, but I really couldn't be bothered about how I presented.

The door opened and I instantly recognised the short, rotund man who walked in. Mr. Collins was Dad's long-time solicitor. He acknowledged Uncle Mo first by saying, "My Lord." Then he turned to us, "Mrs. Triggs, Olivia, Ruth… again may I say how sorry I am for your loss. I have the utmost respe-"

Uncle Mo cleared his throat impatiently and interrupted, "Mr. Collins, enough of that. Let's begin." He then signaled for Mr. Collins to take the empty seat next to me.

Mr. Collins hurried along, he sat down as instructed and then placed his briefcase on his lap and tapped it as he spoke, "My Lord, I have Mr. Triggs' Will and Last Testament here with me…"

"Good. We are ready. You may begin." Uncle Mo's right hand signaled Mr. Collins to continue.

"My Lord, Mrs. Triggs, I'm afraid it is invalid."

Uncle Mo sat up straight and he looked even sterner than usual. "Invalid? What can you possibly mean?"

Mum was also paying close attention now. Even behind her dark Prada sunglasses I could feel her frowning at Mr. Collins.

"I'm afraid there is no longer any wealth to pass on, only debts. Mr. Triggs gambled everything on an investment on a diamond mine in Sierra Leon. It was going to triple his wealth but as in every gamble, sometimes you win, sometimes you lose. Unfortunately, Mr. Triggs borrowed against all his assets to pay for this investment and now the banks are coming to collect…" Mr. Collins continued to explain but I stopped listening as I processed what was just said. We had no money. How could this be? Dad had the Midas touch. My mind whirled with a million questions. Had we lost everything? Our home? Our cars? What was left?

Mum was crying again. Olivia was crying too. So I hugged Mum as she sobbed.

Uncle Mo was standing by now. He paced the floor, his hands behind his back. "Foolish boy. He always thought he was invincible, indestructible. He always thought that the rules didn't apply to him. I knew it was only a matter of time before one of his investments would turn sour. So what's left?"

"Less than twenty thousand pounds in the bank, that is all. But the bank will likely freeze that. The house itself and any non-personal contents and everything else will be turned over to the bank."

Mum cried louder. "Oh what will become of us? Oh Eli, what have you done?" She called out to Dad. "Eli… Eli… why did you leave me?"

Uncle Mo turned to Olivia and I, "Girls, please leave us." It was a command we dared not disobey and after a small nod of agreement from Mum, we left the room. But we stayed just behind the doors where we could still hear everything. We had the right to know our own fate.

Uncle Mo continued, he spat his words as he taunted, "Naomi, look at you, you married for money but you ended up with nothing at the end. Pathetic."

Mum buried her face in her hands. "You must help us. Please. It's what Eli would have wanted. We are your family."

"Yes, for the sake of Eli, I will help my nieces. But not you. You are not family. You never belonged here. You can go back into the hole where you crawled out of. Since my wife died without any children, I am happy to adopt the girls and call them my own. They can continue to live in luxury. I will buy the townhouse from the bank and the girls can continue to call it their home. I'll also pay for their education, for Olivia's arts college tuition and I will pay for Ruth's university expenses and the rent in Cambridge. They'll want for nothing."

My heart stopped as I waited for Mum's answer. I actually wasn't sure what answer I wanted her to give. I didn't want her to give us up yet I didn't want to give everything up! After a few moments of silence,

I heard Mum say, "Thank you. It's what's best for the girls. I appreciate you coming to their rescue." Her voice broke as she finished her response.

My eyes met Olivia's. We stared at each other for what seemed like a very long time. I could see the grief I felt reflected in her eyes and for a moment I felt comforted knowing that I wasn't alone in this. It was a shared grief. A shared loss. We were both broken. We were both overwhelmed

It had obviously taken my mum hours to gather up the fortitude to deliver us the news. It was the afternoon by the time we were finally summoned and we walked into the guest room she was using. Mum was sitting by the window, looking out at the expansive garden.

Maybe she didn't hear us come in because she didn't even look at us to acknowledge that we had arrived. "Mum?" My voice croaked. Even with my own ears I thought I sounded nervous. Admittedly, I was nervous. After all, I knew what my mum was about to say. She was giving us up. Both Olivia and I have had a few hours to process this. Together we discussed the pros and cons. It made so much sense for us to stay with Uncle Mo. But as I looked at Mum at that moment, looking so defeated, so alone, it suddenly made even more sense not to abandon her when she needed us the most. I was at a cross-roads and I really didn't know which way to go.

Mum finally turned her head to look at us. Her eyes were still swollen and tears continued to stream down her cheeks. She opened her arms, a signal for us to come to her. We both ran to her, knelt down in front of her and she embraced us tightly as she continued to cry. "My beautiful girls… this is so hard. Probably the hardest thing I have had to do. It's for the best though and so we must do this. You are to stay with your Uncle Mo. You heard that we have nothing now. Uncle Mo will buy the townhouse and Olivia, you can continue to live there and finish your degree. Ruth, your Uncle Mo will pay for your Cambridge degree and your apartment so you can be with Kane. This is for the best. Yes. It's for the best."

"Mum, are you sure about this? What about you? Will you be alright?" Olivia cried out tearfully.

"I'll be fine. I'll move into my family's old place and I'll get a job. I'll be fine. What's more important is your future. I want you to finish your degree. I want you to live the life you are meant to live. If you stay with me, you'll have nothing. Just promise me that you'll come and visit."

Olivia nodded, "Yes Mum. I promise I'll come to visit."

I watched this interaction. It felt wrong. I knew what I was meant to say. I was supposed to follow suit with a similar interplay as Olivia. But I couldn't make myself say those words. I couldn't abandon my mum. And as the thought formed in my head my resolve to stay with Mum grew and a sense of peace, of doing what was right, settled in my heart. It was a crazy decision. I wasn't prepared for poverty and for the hardship that was sure to come but I also knew that I wasn't prepared to walk away from Mum. So I found myself saying, "Mum, no… please don't ask me to leave you. I want to go with you."

Mum's eyes widened with shock. "Oh Ruth, it's what's best. You have plans that I can't provide for now. I can't afford to send you to Cambridge. I can't afford the lifestyle you've grown accustomed to. You have no idea how hard life is without the privilege you have been so used to. Go with Uncle Mo. Go with your sister. Please."

Olivia's hand tightened on my arm, "You must come with me. Ruth, please."

I ignored Olivia because more and more I knew that this was the right decision. What kind of daughter would I be if I abandoned my own mother in her time of grief and hardship just because it would mean that I could no longer live a life of luxury? With a firmer tone, I reiterated my decision, "Mum, I'm coming with you. I'll go where you go. I'll live where you live. I'm sticking by you Mum, you can't get rid of me."

Mum closed her eyes for a second. Olivia and I waited for her response. When she opened her eyes, she simply looked at me for a second, then two, three, four and then she nodded.

# CHAPTER 3

The five-storey post-war apartment building in Peckham was dwarfed by two massive council tower blocks directly to its right and left. I carried a small box of my belongings as Mum and I climbed the three floors to a peeling light blue door. This was home now. Even before I entered I already knew that it was a far cry to the townhouse I was accustomed to. My mum inserted the key she had been holding in her right hand and as the door opened, she paused and looked at me with a small smile. "Thank you Ruth. Thank you for being here." With those words I knew deep within my soul that I had made the right decision. So I smiled back.

As Mum walked into the flat, I stopped and put the box I was carrying on the floor then reached into my back pocket and I took out my phone. I knew there was something important I needed to do before I stepped into my new home. I took a deep breath and whispered 'Goodbye' as I deleted all my social media accounts and then removed the apps from my phone. The girl in those social media profiles was the old me. It was my old life. It wasn't me anymore. Besides, it would be too difficult for me to see all my old friends moving on without me. With another deep breath and a mix of relief and mourning, I put my phone back in my pocket, picked up the box and stepped through the door.

My grandparents' two-bedroom flat had definitely seen better days. The walls were decent enough if you liked bright yellow and green wallpaper. The carpet I assumed was also green but now just looked faded brownish grey and the kitchen was frozen in time from the 1970's. It was a tiny space but it was livable and besides there was only the two of us. We didn't need much space.

It was another two weeks after the funeral before we could move in to the flat to allow time for the tenants to move out. It gave us time to pack our belongings and choose some furniture to take with us. Looking around this space though, our furniture definitely would look at odds with this place.

In those two weeks I also had to break the news to Kane that I wasn't going to Cambridge with him. He didn't take it well, which of course was not surprising. I wouldn't take it well either, had the situation been reversed. We had it all figured out and here I was flaking out on him. He walked away - stormed away - from me without even a backwards glance. Yet I felt nothing when he walked away. And even though Eve and the rest of the gang had gone MIA on me these past few weeks as well, I didn't feel sad or angry. My heart was already broken so I guess it couldn't be broken any further. The hardest part was saying goodbye to Olivia. Had none of this happened, I would have had to say goodbye anyway when I moved to Cambridge and in fact I was actually living closer to her now than I would have been but we both knew this was different. We were taking different paths. We both knew Uncle Mo. Sooner or later he would demand that Olivia stopped seeing us.

A knock on the door startled me out of my reverie. Three buff men crowded the small doorway. The movers had arrived. "Are you ready for us to bring up your stuff?"

Mum and I answered, "Yes" in unison.

The move took all day as the men navigated the small staircase and small doorways. Finally, the elegant furniture, furnishings and white goods were all in their place. The flat still looked miserable. The wallpaper needed to go. When we had a little bit of money I would suggest to Mum that we needed to refurbish.

Five days later it became apparent that if we needed money to come our way that it wasn't going to come from my mum getting a job. In fact, she hadn't even left her room, let alone the flat. It was all up to me, I needed to get a job. But what job could someone like me get? I had never worked a day in my life! I had no real skills. I had never been very good at anything useful. But I needed to do something. What limited money we had was going to run out and we would starve. Dampening any doubts and fears, I showered and dressed in the nicest conservative dress I could find in my wardrobe – a navy blue Chanel silk dress – and I caught the underground to Harrod's. I loved fashion, surely I could get a job selling clothes?

I walked into the women's fashion department and was immediately attended to by a beautiful sales woman with a blonde bob and perfect make-up. "Good afternoon, how can I help you today?" Her tone was friendly but formal.

"I'm actually looking for a job." I said in the most confident tone I could muster.

Her expression changed with my words. Her face tightened and she frowned as she looked at my dress, my Manolo shoes and my Givenchy bag. "Oh, you certainly look good. We're currently not hiring but leave me your CV, we possibly will have something if someone leaves – maybe in a few months."

CV? Blood drained from my face from sheer embarrassment. Of course I needed a CV to get a job! Why didn't I think of that? I felt so stupid as I explained to her that I didn't have one.

The woman straightened her shoulders and shook her head, "By the looks of you, I can tell you're a riches to rags story. Let me give you a piece of valuable advice. I see your kind come in and out of this store all the time. You think that you're better than everyone. Well let me tell you something, there are a lot of people like me that work our arses off to be able to get a job in places like this. You can't just come in here and expect that just because you're gorgeous and have shopped here before that you'll be great at this job. Go figure out what you're actually good for and then write your CV." And with those words she turned her back on me and walked away.

I was horrified and I was tempted to call her superior to complain but as nasty as she was, she was right. How could I think that I could do this job just because I loved clothes and loved shopping?

Embarrassed and decidedly put in my place, I rushed out of there and I headed back home.

Worry grew inside of me, a monster fed by a dose of reality served up by the sales lady. Throughout my journey back to our flat, this monster grew bigger and nastier. What would happen to Mum and I if I couldn't get a job? Maybe Uncle Mo – no, I stopped myself immediately at that thought. We couldn't rely on Uncle Mo. No, I needed to find a job. Maybe Eve's Dad could get me a job in his company? I dialled Eve's number as I sat in the tube and again it went straight to voicemail. I left her a message but I knew that she was never going to return it. Eve was fickle, she always had been. She was there only during the good times. I tried all my other close friends but no one answered their phones – deliberately, for sure. These were the same girls with their phones permanently attached to their hands. They never missed a call that they wanted to take.

Later, I walked back up the stairs to our flat thinking about what I could put on my CV. Nothing. I'd never even contributed to any charity or causes. No, I had wasted my time on parties and that was not something I could include on a CV! I had no real talent, unlike Olivia who was an amazing painter. At age ten she was already showing at a local gallery and as she matured, so did her talent. Nor was I like Kyle who whizzed through school as a mathematics and science genius and was accepted into pre-med even before he sat his exams. Me, on the other hand, had neither ambition nor talent. I was so hopeless that Dad had to "buy" my admission into Cambridge to study History. No, the only thing going for me was that I was considered pretty and that I was rich. And now, I wasn't even rich.

As I reached the door to our flat, our neighbour's door opened and a pretty middle-aged Asian lady walked out. She smiled when she saw me, a big friendly smile, which at that very moment was a very, very welcome sight. "Hi, you must be my new neighbour! I'm so sorry we haven't met until now but I've been doing double shifts at work the past week. I'm Nora, by the way." She held out her right hand to shake mine.

I immediately liked her cute American accent. In fact, I immediately liked her. I walked over to shake her hand and I smiled back. She was a tiny lady, only reaching up to my shoulders but she had a strong presence. Her pixie cut hair accentuated her friendly eyes that were shining with unabashed curiosity.

I answered, "Hi Nora. I'm Ruth. I live with my mum, Naomi. It's nice to meet you."

"Well when I have the night off, you and your Mum must come over for dinner. I live alone and have no one to cook for but I love cooking. I can make you the best Filipino dish you've ever tasted."

I had no idea what Filipino food was like but my mouth was already watering at the thought of a home-cooked meal. I smiled apologetically as I confessed, "I don't think I've ever had Filipino food before."

"No? Well that's why it will be the best, you'll have nothing to compare it to!" She laughed loudly and whole-heartedly. Her warmth continued to draw me in and I laughed along with her. It was the first time I had laughed since…

"I can't wait to try it." I said honestly.

"Saturday night." She clapped her hands once and continued, "I have the night off. You and your mum must come over. Look, I'm sorry but I better go, I need to get to work." She turned and locked her door. "We are so busy at the moment. We are down a couple of people because I've had two resignations just in the past week. One decided to elope to Paris with her French lover. I know, very romantic but very inconsiderate, she could have at least given us notice. And the other one was just lazy – actually that one I'm not sorry to lose…"

As Nora straightened her light grey blazer and settled her bag on her right shoulders, it occurred to me that this meeting was by no means an accident. It was fate. "I'm looking for a job. I really need it. My mum and I are desperate for money. We lost everything when my Dad died a few weeks ago. My mum is still grieving and can't get out of bed, so it's all up to me." The words rushed out of my mouth and Nora paused as she looked up at me with her warm brown eyes.

"You poor thing. That must be hard. You must still be grieving yourself. Look, I am more than happy to give you a job but let me warn you that it's not an easy job. I work for a boutique hotel as the housekeeping supervisor. So you'll be part of the housekeeping team which means you'll need to clean the rooms, change bed sheets, clean toilet bowls – all the stuff that I'm guessing you've never had to do before-"

"But all the stuff that I'm having to do now. Please, I really do need a job." I was begging. But I didn't care. I had no experience, no true friends to help me out, and suddenly here was an opportunity!

"Ok, Ruth. I'm going to help you. How old are you? Sixteen, seventeen? You're around the same age as my daughter. She's still in the Philippines with my son. I miss her so much! I miss them both. I think I'm going to adopt you and help you. Meet me here tomorrow at six-thirty in the morning and I will take you to the hotel and you can start your first shift then."

Relief washed over me. A mere few minutes ago, I worried about getting a job, yet suddenly I had one! Oh so grateful, I hugged Nora tightly. "Thank you, thank you! I'll work hard, I promise!"

She laughed again and hugged me back. "Ok, I really do have to go now. See you tomorrow!"

I ran into our flat and into Mum's room to deliver the news. The curtains were still down and Mum was still in bed, with her eyes swollen and her nose red, it was obvious she'd been crying again. "Mum, I've got good news! The woman next door just offered me a job! I'll be working in a hotel cleaning rooms. We'll have income! Isn't that great?"

I immediately regretted delivering the words when I saw my mum's sorrowful reaction. This was not welcome news to her. Of course it wasn't. I should have known. I'd been so focused on the income that I forgot how humbling these circumstances were to our family. We were the guests staying in hotels once, now I was going to be the one cleaning after the guests. Mum didn't say a word. She just cried again and turned her back to me.

"Mum, it's going to be fine. We need this. I don't mind the work. I promise you." I really didn't expect an answer as I hopped onto a small occasional chair facing the bed. My eyes focused on the wallpaper that was peeling in the corners and noted how her elegant four-poster bed sat regally and incongruously in the shabby room, taking up most of the available space.

We sat there in silence until it was time for me to prepare dinner. Our staple – ham, cheese and tomato sandwich for lunch as well as dinner. It was the only thing I knew how to make. Tomorrow after work, I planned to go and get some groceries. There were some recipes on YouTube that even someone as hopeless as me, could follow. Now that I had a job, we could afford to get some real food.

# CHAPTER 4

*V*ery early the next day, I found myself walking into The Warner Hotel in Mayfair with Nora. The luxurious boutique hotel sat close to Green Park and not too far from our townhouse. The Warner, converted from a row of Georgian townhouses, had always been one of my favourite places to hang out with friends, particularly for their famous afternoon tea. I loved the decadent leather and velvet furnishings, marble floors and wooden panels. It was everything a London boutique hotel should be and much more.

My steps faltered as I looked around to see if there were any familiar faces. What if I bumped into someone I knew? How embarrassing would it be to serve someone I used to be friends with? No, it was still too early, surely?

Nora stopped and her face softened. She grabbed my hand and pulled me into a doorway that led to a staff only area. "I don't need to be Sherlock Holmes to see that you've come from money – I'm guessing you used to come here as a guest and now you're worried you'll bump into someone you know?"

Embarrassed that Nora read me so easily, I merely nodded.

"It's gonna be fine Ruth. The best thing about housekeeping is that you're more like a ghost. You hardly interact with guests and when you do, it will be only with guests that are staying here which are mostly out of towners or tourists. Besides, we entered through the front so I could show you the hotel. Other times, you'll enter from the back. It'll be fine."

Nora was right. None of my friends would likely stay in the hotel. They'd eat and drink here but it would be unlikely that they would stay in the hotel. I felt a little braver so I nodded and smiled. "Ok, what now?"

Nora clapped her hand once in delight, "That's my girl! Okay let's get you a uniform and then I'll get you to shadow Joy – she's the best – she'll show you what needs to be done."

A little over an hour later, my hair was pulled up in a tight ponytail and I was dressed in a light grey housekeeping uniform with lace frills around the collar. Joy and I entered the second room that needed cleaning. "Alrighty then, Ruth, you can get started with the bed – just like I showed you." Joy, whose name, I quickly learnt, was incongruent to her general demeanor, was a firm woman in her early thirties with brown hair, freckles and an average build. Everything about Joy's appearance screamed average. Except she wasn't. Even in the short space of time I spent with her I could tell that she had a strong personality. She was tough and driven. I could learn a lot from her.

My heart was pounding as I walked towards the bed. I whispered a little prayer, "Oh please let me remember what to do." I stripped the bed and headed to the trolley that was sitting just outside the room for fresh sheets. Once I had them, I walked into the room and I could hear Joy cleaning the bathroom. I focused all my energies into remembering exactly what Joy had shown me, I followed it step by step. When Joy walked out of the bathroom she surveyed the bed clinically. "Okay, pretty good for your first go. You need to be mindful of the edges like this…"

We cleaned another three rooms before it was time for a short break. I was walking to the staff room when I spotted Nora who was beaming a huge smile my way. "You've survived the morning! I'm proud of you!"

I laughed, trying not to show her how tired I already felt. I was sore everywhere and felt muscles I never even knew existed. I put on a brave face and faked a cheery tone, "Bring it on!"

"Good to hear. Hey, I need to run – wait, actually I need a favour please. I have to go and placate a guest who's complaining but I need to check who cleaned her room yesterday. Are you able to go to my office and grab the print out on my desk and bring it to room 201? She's creating quite a ruckus so I need to get there now. My office is in that next hallway to your right and it's the sixth door to your left. Thanks!" Nora was already running as she yelled directions.

Eager to help, I headed to the end of the corridor and turned right. Then I stopped when I couldn't remember the next lot of instructions. Was that sixth door to my left or right? Or maybe it was the fifth door? I groaned in frustration. Then groaned louder when I saw that none of the doors were labeled. Why wouldn't they label them? They were all just plain ecru and they all looked exactly alike! I opened a door to my right and saw a print out on the desk. Pleased that I got it right on the first try, I walked in and the door automatically closed firmly behind me. I picked up the print out and quickly realised it was the wrong print out when the heading said, "Acquisition Contract". I may be new but there was no way a Housekeeping Supervisor would be looking at Acquisition Contracts.

I returned the print out on the desk and sighed as I turned around to leave but suddenly I heard a voice just outside the door. It was a man's voice and he seemed to be on the phone because I could only hear the one voice.

Oh my god, I shouldn't be in this office. I was going to get caught trespassing! I was going to get fired on my first day on the job! This could not be happening! I couldn't afford to lose this job! My heart was pounding and I started to sweat. I was in a panicked state. I had a split second to react as I could hear the man turning the door handle. In the corner of my eye I spotted the closet just to my left so in that moment I made the decision to hide. The closet was empty except for a few hangers, but I had to crouch down to fit in. Hopefully the man would only stay a few minutes and when he left I could then sneak out.

As soon as I closed the closet door, the office door opened. I could hear the man on the phone clearly, "Yes, Mason, Father is interested in acquiring the property but it needs to be at a fair price." I heard him moving around the office. "That's ridiculous, the façade needs a lot of work and don't get me started with the interior." More movement and my heart stopped when I realised his voice was getting closer. Suddenly the closet door opened and my eyes locked with shocked grey eyes.

The man was young. He was also tall and sported an immaculately cut dark brown hair and tailored-fitted dark blue pants, white long-sleeved shirt and a blue tie. He was holding his matching suit jacket, obviously he was planning to hang that in the closet. I should have thought of that. But I didn't. So here I was, caught red-handed and surely was about to get fired.

"Mason, I'll need to call you back." He touched his ear pod to hang up.

I automatically went into survival mode. Still crouched in the closet I looked up at this gorgeous man and I explained myself hurriedly, "So sorry. I got lost, you see, I'm supposed to pick up something from Nora's office but instead I ended up here. I couldn't remember whether she said sixth door on the left or right and there's no names on the doors – why don't you have that? It will really help. Anyway, I got lost and when I heard you coming in I panicked and I hid and I know it's stupid but I really did panic and I guess you do stupid things when you panic. I promise you I wasn't doing anything illegal."

The man nodded but didn't say a thing, instead he extended his hand to offer his assistance to get me out of the closet. I took his hand, it was warm and I didn't know why, maybe from fear or utter embarrassment, but I suddenly lost my breath as he pulled me gently out of the closet.

"Am I in trouble? Gosh, I can't believe I'm in trouble already. It's my first day on the job. I can't believe I'm getting fired on my first day. Who gets fired on their first day…?" I was rambling. But I couldn't stop myself. It must be from desperation; I really did need this job! It had to be that because surely it couldn't be that this man was unnerving me with just how gorgeous he was. I was so used to being surrounded by handsome men. Yet there I was, staring, nervous and rambling on like a maniac.

When he finally spoke, his voice was warm, calm and possibly even slightly amused, "You're not getting fired. We all make mistakes. We all get lost – especially on our first day. I'm Beau Warner by the way. And you are…?" He started shaking my hand and it was only then that I remembered that he was still holding my hand. But it was his name that made me pull my hand away like I had been stung and I took a huge step back. Warner. As in owner of The Warner Hotel! Of all people, why did it have to be a Warner that would find me hiding in their closet? I felt my face go beetroot red.

"Thank you sir for not firing me. I have to go. Nora would be looking for me."

I was hurrying away when I heard him say, "Her office is across the hall." So I ran across the hall and I was relieved when I found the print out sitting on her desk. I ran to find Nora, hoping never to encounter Beau Warner ever again.

The rest of the day was hard. Cleaning rooms was grueling physical work. It was nothing like I had ever done before. I remembered how I used to complain about PE or whenever I had to walk any great distance. This was a million times worse. And it was only Day One.

It was mid-afternoon when my shift ended. I was walking out of the hotel when Nora called out for me to wait. She caught up to me and winked. "So you're getting the boss' attention already and it's only your first day."

My eyes widened in panic. Great, I was going to lose my job after all! "Oh no! What did he say? It was a horrible mistake-"

Nora laughed and she reached up and patted me on my shoulder, "Calm down Ruth. I'm just being cheeky. Beau came looking for me wanting to know your name and he was asking a lot of questions. So are you single? Because if you are, he's quite a catch! Not only is he cute, his Dad owns the hotel, and they have a couple more – one in Barcelona and in Vienna. Rumour is that they're going to open one in Athens. He's smart too, you know, he's finishing his business degree in Oxford. On his days off he co-manages the hotel. Been working in the hotel since he was a kid. I can set you up-"

I shook my head vehemently, "No, no, please, don't! That's the last thing I need right now. Besides, I haven't officially broken it off with my boyfriend, Kane. I know he loves me so I'm hoping once he gets over the fact that I didn't follow through on our plans that he'll take me back. Anyways, let me tell you the real reason Mr. Warner's asking about me and it's not because he's interested in me..." We started walking to the tube station as I relayed what was the most embarrassing moment of my life.

Nora was crying with laughter and was in hysterics by the time I finished my story. "You my girl," She said between giggles, "is just what I need in my life right now!" She kept laughing and by the end of our conversation, I was laughing too because it was true what they say – laughter was contagious.

As we climbed the stairs heading to our flat, Nora suddenly stopped and looked at me thoughtfully. "You know, the questions Beau was asking about you makes me think that he's interested. He wanted to know everything I knew about you."

I couldn't believe it. After all, why would someone like Mr. Warner be interested in a mere housekeeper? "Stop match-making Nora. This is a lost cause." Despite how handsome Beau was, I was still very much in love with Kane and I knew he still loved me. It was only a matter of time before his temper cooled off and he would come calling. "I told you, I have a boyfriend." I smiled innocently and kept climbing up the stairs.

Nora rushed to catch up to me, "Are you sure? Because if you're not interested in rich, tall, dark and handsome, how about poor, tall, blonde and handsome? There's someone else asking about you. Jake, the bartender, he's a cutie but a bit of a playboy but you may be the one to tame him…"

I shook my head and smiled at her relentless matchmaking. I was relieved when we finally made it to our floor. "I'll see you tomorrow, Nora!"

# CHAPTER 5

*I* grimaced when I felt pain shoot through my shoulders as I pulled the dirty sheets off the king size bed. Even after five weeks, my body was still constantly sore from cleaning but today I was actually grateful for that pain because it kept my mind off the fact that it was the two-month anniversary of the passing of Dad, Kyle and Mark. Two months since this pain in my heart started and it hadn't abated since. Two months since our world was turned upside down and thrown into chaos. Two months since everything changed.

I felt my phone vibrate in my pocket. I quickly lowered the sheets so I could read the incoming text message – it was from Olivia. We'd been in constant contact including daily phone calls and text messages. She seemed to be happy living by herself with the servants in the big house while she continued to party with her friends. Sometimes she also delivered me news that she'd heard in the grapevine or stalked on social media about Kane. The latest was that he had started seeing someone else he met at Cambridge, a Scottish Socialite, or so I was told. That was a couple of weeks ago and I was devastated when she told me. I was so sure he would come to the realisation that this was the right decision for me and eventually would support me. I was being a good daughter, after all. My mum needed me right now because even after two months, she still wasn't eating properly and she still hardly left the bed let alone the flat. Someone needed to look after her.

Olivia's text message flashed again as I unlocked my phone to read it, "Enough of this, it's been two months. You need to come home." It wasn't really a new message from Olivia. She had sent me a text message to leave Mum and to come home to her every single day.

I messaged back, "I told you, Mum can't even get out of bed. She needs me."

Olivia quickly messaged back, "She'll be forced to if you're not there as her servant at her beck and call."

I answered, "I'm not her servant. I'm her daughter."

I waited for a reply for a minute but Olivia didn't answer back. I might have offended her with that comment and I started to regret the text, but it was the truth. Despite how hard life had been in the past weeks, I knew this was exactly where I needed to be. And despite the aching body after every single shift or the long nights sitting with Mum as she continued to mourn for Dad and the boys, I knew I couldn't just walk away and choose the easy route.

I heard a noise by the doorway and saw Joy standing there. There was not an ounce of joy in her expression, her lips were twisted and her hands were on her hips, "Ruth, I just checked the rooms you've just done and you haven't refilled the amenities! The toilet's not cleaned properly as well. I know you're Nora's friend but that doesn't mean you can get away doing a sub-standard job. I've had to redo those rooms. You better get better or I'm going to have to talk to Nora." And with that, Joy huffed away.

I was already feeling low and the set down Joy just delivered was the final blow that succeeded in knocking me down. It really was all too hard! I was good for nothing! I was an awful sister and lo and behold, I was also an awful housekeeper. Dejected, my knees gave way and I found myself sitting on the bed.

It wasn't too long, maybe only a few seconds, before I heard another noise by the door. This time it was Jake, the bar tender. He always looked like he'd just stepped out of a Rolling Stones magazine. With his long blonde hair and piercing green eyes, he seriously looked like a rockstar. Most of the female staff was half in love with him and the word was that he had dated at least half of them. He had made such a deliberate effort to catch me at every single break time since I started, but he was sweet, was so easy to talk to and was hilariously funny so we had formed an easy friendship. Besides, admittedly, I was flattered by the attention he showered me. "Hey, I just heard what Joy said as I was walking here to find you. Are you okay?"

His soft tone was such a welcome one after Joy's that I found myself wanting to confide in him, despite my instincts yelling at me to ask him to leave. "No. Actually, I'm not okay." It had been a hard day and I needed a friend.

Jake walked into the room, closed the door and sat down on the edge of the bed next to me. "Don't worry about Joy. She takes everything far too seriously. It's because she doesn't have a boyfriend so she's frustrated and she takes it out on everyone." It was obviously a joke designed to make me smile but it didn't work.

"It's not just that. Today is two months since I lost three very special people in my life. My mum is home alone and she's probably crying her lungs out. And I think my sister is mad at me. And as you heard, I'm hopeless at my job." Tears pricked my eyes but they didn't come out. Truth be told, I still hadn't cried since that day two months ago.

Jake made an empathetic noise and put his arms around me. It felt good to be comforted. It felt good to know someone cared. I had been the one doing all the comforting the past two months; it felt nice to be the one on the receiving end. I laid my cheek on his shoulders and we sat just like that for a few moments. I didn't stop him when he started rubbing my back, it felt good to know I had a friend. I closed my eyes, resting in his embrace.

It was some time later that I realised that Jake's other hand was now sitting on the base of my neck and it was moving slowly looking for the zip to my uniform. By then I could hear his ragged breathing. Embarrassed that I gave the wrong impression, I pulled away but Jake's hands closed tightly onto my forearms, locking me close to him. "Don't go." It wasn't a suggestion. It sounded more like a command. His voice was no longer friendly and his eyes looked crazed.

"Jake, I'm sorry if I have mis-led you. We're friends, that's all." I tried to pull away again but he was much stronger than me and he kept me locked in place.

"No, you're playing games. Stop acting like you don't want me. I know you do." He then grabbed hold of my upper arms and he pulled me down roughly on the bed, his whole body pinned me down.

My survival instinct kicked in – there was no way I was going to be raped by this man! I started screaming and kicking and pushing. He was trying to kiss me and his right hand was pulling my uniform up as his muscled body continued to pin me down.

Even in my distress, I could hear someone trying to get into the locked room. I screamed louder, this time calling for help as I tried to wriggle away from Jake's hold.

I heard the disgusting sound of material ripping and I realised as I felt air on my shoulders and stomach that Jake had ripped my uniform from its collar. I started punching him but nothing I did deterred him. He had complete power over me. Fear washed over me as it dawned on me that this man, who I thought was a friend, was determined to hurt me. And I was powerless to stop him.

Suddenly I felt Jake being lifted from me and next thing I knew he was on the ground unconscious. Beau was standing over him, he looked angry but his face softened a little when he turned to me, "Ruth…"

I sat up, somewhat conscious that I was half naked in front of the boss. I tried lifting up my torn dress to cover myself. I couldn't look at Beau. I was ashamed. This was entirely all my fault – I allowed Jake into the room, I gave him the wrong impression. I put myself in this situation. I deserved this. "I'm so sorry." I apologised, appalled, embarrassed that I had yet again put myself in a situation where I could get fired.

Beau knelt down in front of me until we were face to face. Anger was etched in his face but as I looked deeper into his eyes I could also see concern. "Ruth, I should be the one apologising. Everyone that works here should have the right to be safe. Better still, every woman has the right to go about their business without fear of assault. This is not your fault."

I looked away, too ashamed to face him. "But I may have led him on without meaning to. I thought we were friends, you see and I'm having an awful day and he was comforting me…"

"He took advantage of you. Jake's fired. You never have to see him again. I'm reporting him to the police. What he's done is unacceptable and it's criminal. Please, don't blame yourself. The only person at fault here is him."

At that moment, Nora came running into the room and she enveloped me into her arms. "That bastard, I can't believe he's done this…"

Beau straightened up. "I'll leave you in Nora's capable hands. The police and ambulance are on their way." I was about to protest to say that I was okay but he stopped me, "I want you checked up to make sure you really are okay." He then turned around and walked towards Jake who by now was awake and was groaning in pain. "I'll deal with this one and wait for the police downstairs." I turned my head away, so not to catch Jake's eyes as he was led away.

The hour that followed was a complete blur as the EMT examined me and gave me the all clear. They said that I was lucky that Beau came when he did. That I was lucky because apart from the bruises, I was going to be okay. I almost laughed at the absurdity of what they were saying. Lucky? I didn't feel lucky. What kind of luck did I have that my Dad and brothers should all die because of some drunk driver? Oh, and how lucky was I that my Dad had lost all our money and now we lived in poverty and that I had to work in a hotel as a housekeeper? And yes, I must have hit the jackpot that Jake had zeroed in on me just as I was feeling vulnerable. Oh yes, I was one very lucky lady.

A female officer walked into the room just as the EMT were walking out. She asked me for a statement and I described what happened. By now I was feeling exhausted and overwhelmed and was wishing I could just go home and tuck myself into bed for days and just forget about the world. Maybe Mum had the right idea after all.

After a few photos were taken of me by the police officer, I was finally able to shower and change to my clothes.

Nora stayed close to me the whole time. And later, she also took me home in a cab and tucked me into bed. Mum didn't even come out of her room when we arrived and I was relieved that I didn't have to explain what had just happened.

I curled into bed, I wanted to sleep but every time I closed eyes, my mind continued to replay the episode over and over again. So I was grateful that Nora offered to stay with me. And because I couldn't sleep yet, I ended up sharing everything that my family had been through the past couple of months. I narrated the story like it was someone else's life. And Nora followed suit. She shared how hard it was to be living away from her two children. They were living with their Dad's family in the Philippines and all her money went towards their education, their clothes and other necessities. She also mentioned that Mr. Warner was working with an immigration lawyer to get her daughter and son to the UK. We talked until late and until my eyes finally closed and I drifted off to sleep.

# CHAPTER 6

# BEAU WARNER

*A*nger continued to overwhelm me as I sat in my father's office the very next day. We were there to discuss what happened and how we could support Ruth. I couldn't get the picture of that bastard on top of Ruth out of my head, and the picture of her, torn disheveled and blaming herself for what that ass did. As satisfying as it was to punch the guy unconscious, I wished I could have done much more damage.

"... And how is the poor girl?" Genuine concern was written all over my father's face. In business, Israel Warner was not one to trifle with. He had a reputation for being cold, cunning, ruthless and determined to get his way. Only his family knew what was really hidden behind the mask. He was a man who cared deeply, especially for those he loved.

Nora sat next to me and she answered the question posed by my father. "Sir, she's doing okay considering. I've given her the week off. But you know I do feel for her. Yesterday was the second month anniversary of her father and brothers' deaths. They died in a car accident in Peru while on holiday. She really didn't need this, the poor girl."

My father's eyes widened and blood drained from his face. "Hold on, it would be too much of a coincidence for it to be another family... Is Ruth's last name Triggs?"

"You know her?" I questioned my father, interested in what he had to say.

He sat back in his chair, "I don't know her, but I knew her mother. Naomi and I went to school together and I knew she married Eli Triggs. I did see his death and his sons' deaths reported all over the news a couple of months ago and wondered how Naomi was doing. But he's rich. He had lucrative investments so I don't understand why their daughter would have to work. They should be set up for life."

Ruth came from money and my father knew her mother – what were the odds? Shocked at this dual revelation, I had so many more questions whirling in my head but before more questions could be asked, Nora answered, "I know why Sir. Ruth said that her father lost all their money because he put everything on one investment that went bad. Her Uncle still has money but he hates her Mum so he threw her out. Ruth and her sister had the choice to be adopted by their Uncle or go with their mother and Ruth chose to look after her mother but her sister stayed. They've moved back to her mother's old flat, next door to mine, actually. That's how we met."

My father nodded, "I know that flat. I grew up not far from there."

I couldn't believe what I was hearing. I have to admit, my interest was piqued ever since I saw Ruth hiding in my closet. Yes, she was attractive, but there was something more about her that called out to me. But I knew that as a manager I had no business being attracted to an employee so I tried to forget about her, tried to ignore her. Yet I found myself walking through her designated floors on the days she was working just so I could see a glimpse of her. And it was during one of those floor walks that I heard her screams. It made me angrier at the thought that Ruth had been through so much already and now this!

My father turned back to Nora, "And how is Naomi?"

"I don't know Sir. I still haven't met her. She is grieving deeply, from what Ruth has told me. She doesn't leave her room. It's why Ruth is determined to look after her mother even though it means she has to work here and give up her education." I could tell by the way Nora spoke about Ruth that she had grown to care for her.

"I do admire the fact that she has chosen to look after her mum." I found myself saying out loud. "She could have chosen the easy option." Without a doubt, most women I knew would do anything not to have to give up their lavish lifestyle. I found my admiration for Ruth increasing by the minute.

I glanced at my father and saw that he was frowning at me. He actually looked worried. "True, son, but just be careful with this one. I knew her mother and as they say, 'The apple doesn't fall far from the tree'."

I shrugged, hoping that I was effectively pulling off nonchalance, "It's not what you're thinking, Father. She's just an employee, besides I just want to make sure she's well looked after given she was assaulted under our care."

Father continued to frown but he must have decided to leave the topic well alone. Instead he turned to Nora, "Give her another week of paid leave. And if there is anything else she needs – counseling, whatever – let Beau know." With that, Nora was dismissed.

A few minutes later, I found myself being convinced by my father to have coffee with him at the hotel restaurant. The large room emanated the elegance of a classic English dining room and it was one of my favourite rooms in the entire hotel. It was just a few minutes past 2pm so the hotel was nearly empty of the lunch patrons. We sat by the window on two large leather chairs, sipping black coffee. We talked business for a few more minutes then my father grew silent, obviously deep in thought.

"Father, everything okay?" I inquired softly. Something was up.

"Yes son. I think I am still shocked that one of Naomi's daughters is working here." Then he looked me in the eye and said, "I might as well tell you… Naomi and I were not simply schoolmates, we dated throughout high school and university. I was very much in love with her but she left me for Eli Triggs, the youngest son of a very wealthy Baron. Not many people know this, but during that time I worked overtime every single day at the local grocery store to be able to afford a small engagement ring. When I finally saved up enough money, I was so excited. I bought it in the morning and planned to propose to her at dinner that night. The only saving grace is that she broke it off with me before I had the chance to propose. I didn't know she was seeing another man behind my back, so while I was breaking my back working non-stop to save up for our future, she was busy securing her future with someone else. I was so angry." Even years later, I could still hear an undertone of hurt and anger.

I shook my head in empathy, "What did you do?" I couldn't even imagine how heartbreaking that would have been for my father.

"I decided that I was going to be rich and she would come to regret her decision. From that day I became determined to succeed. I sold the ring, used it to enroll in a hotel management course and the rest is history." The history of his career was familiar to me. His course facilitator had contacts in The Savoy and my father started working there as a trainee. He eventually became the assistant manager and through the hotel he met an Arab Sheikh who he partnered up with and they bought a small hotel together. From there my father's wealth grew until he was able to afford to buy his own hotels. "I guess you can say I have Naomi to thank for all this. If she hadn't turned me down, I probably wouldn't have all this."

He grew quiet again. It seemed like he still harboured some resentment for Naomi's betrayal.

I was grateful for the silence as I contemplated Ruth's journey. How hard it must be for her to go from rich and care-free to poor and full of care. She was one strong character. I admired that.

My father's phone rang, shaking us both out of our contemplation. He looked down at his phone and smiled, "It's your sister. I better answer this. She's wanting me to organise her next on the job training. Don't forget – your mother is expecting you for dinner tonight!" He quickly stood up and walked towards his office.

I smiled as my eyes tracked his progress out of the restaurant. My father was a push-over when it came to the women in his life. My father obviously recovered well enough from the heartache inflicted by Ruth's mother. He met my mother while she was dining at The Savoy with some friends and according to their narrative, they immediately hit it off and were inseparable ever since. Once they married she became a stay-at-home wife and mother and ran practically every committee there was at school and at church. And no matter how busy my father was, if my mother asked him to drop everything, he did. And Steph, now fifteen years old, was my father's pride and joy. She knew exactly what she wanted out of life and she wasn't afraid to ask my father for help in getting her there. Case in point, her ambition was to be a lawyer hence my father had been organising for her to intern at various law firms around town.

I finished my coffee and stood up. It was time to get back to work. I still had an assignment I had to finish before dinner so I needed to make sure I left a little earlier than 5pm today.

However, instead of heading to my office, I found myself in the restaurant kitchen looking for our executive chef, Leon. An idea had formed and I was determined to follow it through. I found Chef Leon in his office, contemplating the menu.

"Monsieur Warner, how can I help you?" He asked warmly as he shook my hand in greeting.

"Leon, I need a favour. There is a housekeeping staff member who's currently on leave. When she gets back, I need you to 'accidently' bump into her and somehow offer her food to take home. They are struggling to get food on the table so her and her mother probably haven't eaten decent food in months. I don't think she will accept blatant charity but if you make it seem like it is excess food that would be thrown out anyway then I'm sure she'll accept it. Bill me personally for the meals. I'll email you her details."

Leon smiled warmly in agreement, "Why of course! Do you know what food she loves? I can make her something special every night!"

"Thank you, Leon. I'm sure whatever is on special that night will do nicely. Thank you again, my friend." I turned to exit but paused as I remembered that Leon had a reputation of not being able to keep his mouth shut. "Please, do make sure you don't mention that I have anything to do with this."

He laughed and made the motion of zipping his lips shut.

I nodded and walked away, very pleased with myself.

# CHAPTER 7

The wind blustered around me as I ran towards the staff entrance of The Warner. I'd been back at work for three days now after the two-week break that Nora and the Warners kindly provided. They also offered counselling sessions, which I refused. No, the break was exactly what I needed and it gave me time to strip that awful wallpaper off the walls in our flat and repainted it a nice neutral eggshell-white. The best news was that Mum actually got out of her room to help out. We had a nice time chatting and laughing as we realised that it was the blind leading the blind. We really had no idea how to go about painting the flat! Yet we did it, we painted the entire flat and it looked so much better. It was starting to feel like home.

Now back at work, I was determined to act like the assault never happened. I forced myself to get back to routine. Except for when I had to clean that room for the first time. Thankfully Joy was so understanding about the situation and offered to clean that room for me in perpetuity. Apart from that slight hiccup, I was sure that I had successfully put that episode behind me and I was proud of myself. I was fast becoming an expert in being able to set emotions aside and carry on.

And everyone at work had been so nice when I got back. Yes, Joy was a lot nicer to me and even Leon, the hotel executive chef, whom I had never met, sought me out and offered to give me their excess food after every shift. So, on most nights, Mum and I had been feasting on Michelin star French cuisines! Beau had also been kind enough to check up on me and of course, Nora was an amazing support throughout, even as far as helping paint the flat during her days off.

I walked into the staff common room and greeted everyone that was there. A few minutes later I rushed to get to the first floor I was to clean that morning. It hadn't been fifteen minutes before I heard my name being called through the radio. I answered, "Ruth here."

It was Nora. "Ruth, Room 311 has asked for two extra towels. Can you please action?"

"Sure thing." I answered and immediately rushed to get extra towels from my trolley. I was on the second floor so I decided to take the service stairs rather than the lift. Within a few minutes I was standing in front of Room 311 and knocking on the door, "Housekeeping." I announced loud enough so I could be heard within the room.

The door opened immediately and I was shocked when I saw it was Olivia. "Oh good, it's you! We were hoping you would be the one to come."

Even though my mind was still trying to wrap itself around the fact that my sister - whom I haven't seen for months - was here in front me, I immediately zeroed in on what she had said. "We...?" I inquired. Who was she with?

Olivia opened the door wider and there inside the suite was Kane, smiling that beautiful lop-sided smile that I had always loved. At that moment, I was overcome with joy. I was so happy to see Olivia and Kane. After everything that had happened, it was so good to see two people that brought me back to a time when everything was perfect. When life was fun. I found myself running into Kane's arms and when he cuddled me closer, I felt warm happiness spread throughout my body. And when he kissed me, I kissed him back. I missed him. I missed what we had. I missed being held like this.

"Alright lovebirds, that's enough." Olivia interrupted. I turned to see Olivia visibly annoyed. Of course she was, I hadn't seen her in months, yet I hadn't even given her a hug. I was being a horrible sister. So I immediately walked over to Olivia and I gave her the biggest squeeze I could manage.

"I missed you too big sis! Like I say to you every day, you are very slack not to come and visit us. Uncle Mo doesn't need to know. Mum misses you terribly and I miss you so so so so much."

Olivia stepped back from my embrace. "That's why I'm here, Ruth. Look, I miss you too. We should be together. It's not fair that you have to lower yourself like this."

It was at that moment that I became aware of how dowdy I must look in my housekeeping uniform and hair haphazardly pulled up in a ponytail. I didn't even have any make up on my face. And in contrast, just how beautiful and fashionable Olivia looked; immaculately dressed in her green Gucci long sleeved dress and black designer boots. I then looked at Kane who always looked runway ready. Suddenly, I felt embarrassed. I felt ugly.

Olivia continued, "Please Ruth, enough's enough. You have proven yourself a good daughter. But you need to think about yourself now. When you told me that you were assaulted – nearly raped – I was angry! This is not the life you should be living. It's too much of a sacrifice. It's time to come home, Ruth." Olivia was pleading. This was a big sister looking out for her little sister.

A part of me wanted to go with her and with Kane. Go back to a place where everything was easy. Where I snapped my fingers and it would all be done for me. Go back to Kane. Pick up where we left off like the last three months never happened. I closed my eyes and allowed myself to dream of that alternative universe.

But then I remembered my mum. I remembered her tears, the empty shell she had become and the small glimmer of hope that she was getting better just these last couple of weeks as we worked on the flat together. If I abandoned her now, there was no telling how much farther Mum would retreat into her little world. I couldn't let that happen. I couldn't lose Mum as well. I needed to stay with her. It was the right decision then and it was still the right decision. I took a deep breath before I answered, "I'm sorry Olivia. You know I can't abandon Mum. She needs me."

"I need you! I need you to be the sister I had before all this happened! I need you to stop embarrassing me! I need you to come home!" Olivia was screaming now.

Her words shocked me. Embarrassing her? "What do you mean? How am I embarrassing you?"

"Ruth, come on! You can't be that naïve! You are still in London. People have seen you working here. It's all over social media! Everyone's sharing pics of you in that ugly uniform! It's become a game. Everyone's laughing at you… everyone's laughing at me! This has to stop!"

I knew then that Olivia was not here because of a genuine concern for me. Her genuine concern was for herself. Her reputation. That really hurt. "Oh, so you're here because I'm embarrassing you, not because you miss me and you care for my well-being?"

Olivia's face reddened at being caught out. "Of course I care-"

Kane interceded at that point, probably realising that Olivia had lost her case. "Ruth, babe, it's just not the same without you. Olivia genuinely misses you. I do too, I'm lonely in Cambridge. Please, babe. Please come with us." He walked over to me and slowly pulled me back into his arms. "Let me take you away from this horrible place. I'll protect you. I won't let anyone else hurt you. I promise, your mum will be just fine without you. We can hire a carer so she'll have someone with her. If your Uncle won't pay for it, I'll pay for it. I'll do anything if it means having you with me in Cambridge."

It was a tempting offer. It really was. Maybe a professional carer would be good for Mum, maybe they could better care for her than I could. But my instincts, my gut, was telling me that she needed me and not a stranger. "You don't understand, Kane, Olivia... Mum is getting a little bit better. It's slow, but she is getting better. Just this week she got out of her room and we talked and we laughed a little. She won't do that with a stranger. She misses you Olivia. I know it will really help her if you come and visit." Now I was the one pleading.

But Olivia ignored me. Her lips twisted and she simply asked, "Is this your final answer?"

Confidently and with no ounce of doubt, I uttered, "Yes."

Kane's arms tightened around me, "Babe, Cambridge is so much fun! The parties are epic. You'll love it there. I'm telling you, it's even better than we imagined. Come with me-"

"I can't Kane." I said decidedly, my tone firmer.

"If you're not coming with me, Ruth, then we really are over." His hold slackened as he waited for my answer to his ultimatum.

I lost my breath in that second. I may be young but I recognised that this really was a defining moment in my life. This was a point of no return. All this time I had held out hope that Kane would miss me and come back to me. And he did, but it held conditions. And they were not ones I was willing to take. My voice shook when I answered, "I'm sorry Kane. I really can't leave Mum. If you really loved me, you would understand that and support my decision."

Kane's eyes grew cold as he stepped away from me. "Well, if that is your final answer then there is nothing else to say. Goodbye Ruth."

Olivia cleared her throat and I turned my gaze to her as she sighed, "Ruth, if you won't do it for Kane, do it for me. If you walk away right now, I will no longer have a sister."

I didn't think my heart could break any more. After everything that had happened in the past three months, my heart was already in pieces. Yet Olivia's words shattered whatever was left of my heart and it hurt even more. Indescribable pain. Because while Dad and the boys were gone, they didn't choose to leave but here was my only sister - whom I was closest to - choosing to disown me. "Olivia-"

"Are you coming with us?" Olivia's voice was cold. It was a tone I'd never heard before, never during any of our previous fights. This was different and I knew that this was not a mere threat. She meant it.

I answered again, "No."

Olivia nodded then physically turned her back to me. The unmistakable act of rejection. Dismissal, even.

"Olivia, Kane, please. Mum needs me more than you both could ever need me-"

Olivia walked over to the door and opened it, "Please leave. Goodbye Ruth. As far as I'm concerned, you're gone just like Dad and the boys."

"Olivia, please! Surely you can't mean that! We're sisters! We were so close!" I pleaded but Olivia didn't even bat an eyelid.

"You've made your bed Ruth, now lie in it. Goodbye." Kane shrugged.

Knowing I had truly lost two people I loved, the grief I felt for my Dad and brothers resurfaced and combined with this recent loss and what happened a couple of weeks ago - it all just felt unbearable. Trying to keep my bearings, I straightened my shoulders and walked out of the room but as soon as I was in the hallway, I ran down the stairs. I needed to talk to someone, I needed Nora.

I knocked on her office door, once, twice, three times, no answer. Where could she be? I thought about checking the common room when Beau's office door opened and there he stood, "Ruth?" And when he saw my obvious distress he asked, "What's wrong?" His voice was soft and it was warm and it drew me to him.

I found myself answering without thinking, "Everything. Everything's wrong! Mr. Warner -"

"Call me Beau. Tell me what's wrong, come into my office and we can talk."

I walked into his office and he gestured for me to sit on the pale blue sofa by the window. He took a couple of minutes to prepare me tea and as he handed me the china cup, he smiled gently, "Ok, now we're ready. Tell me what's wrong." He sat down on the matching one-seater, bent forward, rested his elbows onto his knees and waited for me to speak.

And at that point, I wanted to talk. About everything. Here was someone who seemed to genuinely want to listen, someone who seemed to genuinely care. This time, my instincts told me to trust him, that he wasn't like Jake who only wanted to take advantage of me. So I told him everything. From the beginning. When I spoke of my Dad and my brothers' deaths, he held my hand. When I spoke of Kane's rejection, he told me he didn't deserve me. When I spoke of my sister's abandonment, he gave me hope that she would eventually come around. When I spoke of the guilt and fear I carried over the episode with Jake, he helped me realise that it wasn't my fault.

His gentleness made me feel safe and cared for and finally I felt ready to let go of all the emotions that I hadn't known I had bottled up so tightly. And just like a volcano ready to erupt, I felt the tremors in my hands, arms then my whole body. For the first time since that fateful day, I allowed myself to feel. I allowed myself to grieve. I allowed myself to cry. And boy, did I cry!

# CHAPTER 8

When my tears finally dried up and my breathing slowed, an hour had passed. Yet Beau continued to sit with me. His mere presence was a comfort in itself and having cried and acknowledged my heartache, I actually felt a little better. I felt lighter. "I'm so sorry I downloaded on you like that."

Beau directed a friendly frown my way then he smiled a gentle smile, "Don't be silly, Ruth. You are one strong lady to still be standing after everything you've been through. It's only normal that you're still grieving. I'm more than happy to be an ear to listen."

He looked genuine and I believed him. I knew I should be embarrassed that I was sitting here having poured my heart out to my boss' boss, but as I looked into his kind grey eyes, I just knew that we were fast becoming friends. "Thank you, Beau. I really appreciate it."

We smiled at each other for a few moments and then Beau quickly stood up, breaking the connection. "You know what you need? Fresh air! I'll message Nora that you're taking the rest of the day off. Get changed, freshen up and I'll take you out to get some fresh air. It will do you good."

Fresh air sounded exactly like what I needed so I agreed to meet Beau in half an hour in the staff car park. I was glad that the change room was empty, the last thing I needed was anyone inquiring after my tear-stained appearance. I must look a mess. I looked at myself in the mirror, after dressing back into my jeans and a simple long-sleeved black shirt. My face was blotchy, my eyes were red and swollen and my ponytail had collapsed. Whoa, I looked like a mess! I didn't have make up in my bag so all I could do was wash my face and fix my ponytail. I looked better but nothing could hide the fact that I had just been crying. Resigned that this was the best I could do with my appearance, I grabbed my navy blue parka and my Gucci crossover bag and ran to the staff car park.

Beau was already waiting for me when I arrived. He smiled, "I think this is the first time I've seen you without the uniform on."

I felt self-conscious. I knew we were just friends and this was certainly not a date, yet I couldn't help but wished I at least had make up on. "I look like a mess." I stated simply, reddening a little with embarrassment.

Beau shook his head, "You may not look as glamorous as you did every time you stepped into Hacienda, but I like you like this, natural and without being so made-up."

His sentiments warmed me, and I reddened even more. Until it dawned on me that he mentioned the very club that my friends and I frequented. Had he seen me there? No, he said this was the first time he saw me without the uniform and he didn't seem like the type of person to hang at the Hacienda. It was probably a wild guess or could it be that he had searched my name up online where he would have seen my movements documented by social publications? Surely he wouldn't have bothered to look me up though…? As a joke and possibly to gauge his reaction, I playfully said, "How do you know about Hacienda? Have you 'Googled' me?"

Now it was Beau's turn to redden. His whole face turned beetroot red and he just laughed a half-hearted denial and motioned for us to head to his car.

I followed him, intrigued that Beau was curious enough about me that he would go searching online for information about me. The practical side of my brain then kicked in, it was likely that he searched online while I was getting changed. He just listened to my story, after all, and maybe he needed to do his own research to verify my story? Yes, that must be it. And I couldn't blame him. My riches to rags story might seem a little far-fetched to anyone hearing it for the first time.

His car was a little black Alfa Romeo Giulietta. Perfect for city driving. It was practical yet it had a heart. I smiled at how his choice of car reflected what little I knew of Beau. He opened the door for me, "Hop in."

So I did and when he turned on the engine, I asked, "So where are we going?"

He just smiled at me and winked, "Surprise."

Half an hour later we were parking at Tower Hill. I was really curious now. What had he planned for us? "You're showing me the Crown Jewels?" I joked. He laughed then shrugged his shoulders but didn't say a thing.

A few minutes later, we were both rugged up as we walked towards the Tower of London. He stopped at an area barricaded to the public where he then pulled out his phone and spoke to someone, saying, "We're here." A few seconds later we heard a make-shift gate open and a man was calling out to Beau. He looked about the same age as Beau, with brown hair and a friendly smile. "Ruth, this is my good friend Karl. He manages the ice rinks going up all over the city for winter. This one opens next week to the public, but today we're helping Karl out and testing it before it goes live."

Karl patted Beau on the back and then shook my leather-gloved hand as a greeting. "Nice to meet you, Ruth. You guys are all set. The place is ready for you to enjoy. I'll have to leave you for now, I need to check out the Somerset House, that one is running a little behind schedule!" He gestured for us to enter the gate. As soon as we walked in, I was taken aback at how beautiful and inviting the ice rink looked against the medieval walls of the Tower. "Gorgeous." I found myself saying under my breath.

A large clear marquee stood against the ice rink and Karl led us to its door. "Enjoy. I really must run now!" We said our thanks and farewell to Karl and watched as he disappeared out of sight.

Beau then turned to me with a smile, "Shall we?" He gestured toward the marquee entrance. I stepped in and my eyes immediately surveyed what was inside. A week before the season opened, the place was still empty however on a long lone wooden bench was a large picnic basket, a neatly folded picnic rug and a fur blanket. And to the side of the bench were two pairs of ice skates.

I loved ice-skating as a kid. Dad always took us out ice-skating when we were kids. I'd forgotten about that. A rush of sadness lay heavy within my heart as I remembered the fun we had as a complete family unit.

"Are you okay, Ruth?" Beau was in front of me now, noticing that my eyes had welled up.

I nodded as I wiped my eyes with the back of my leather-gloved hands. "I'm, fine. I just remembered how much my family loved ice-skating, once upon a time. When we got older, I guess we just didn't want to ice-skate with our parents anymore. It's been ages, I can't wait to get out there. Let's go!" I sat down on the bench, took my boots off and pulled on the smaller skates. They fit perfectly!

Beau was still pulling his boots on but I couldn't wait. Especially knowing the entire rink was all ours! I opened the marquee flap that led to the rink and stepped into the ice. It was like I never stopped skating. I sped around and around the rink, loving the feel of the chilled breeze on my bare face. I felt light. I felt free.

As I was taking another lap around the rink, I saw Beau standing hesitantly by the entrance. I stopped in front of him. "Come in. I'll race you."

His face was priceless, half fear, half pride as he held onto the sides of the entrance with his dear life. I couldn't believe it. Could it be that Beau, who seemed so capable at everything, actually didn't know how to skate? I found myself warming up to the fact that he wasn't perfect, after all. "You don't know how to skate, do you? But why did you take me here?"

Beau shrugged, still holding on tightly to the railing. "I'm asking myself the very same thing right now, believe me! I don't know, I just knew you would love it here. So go! Skate. I'll figure out how to get myself onto the ice without ending up on my arse."

I laughed, enjoying this show of vulnerability. "Lucky you, I'm a great teacher! I taught Mark how to ice-skate." I held out my gloved hands, "Trust me."

He stared into my eyes as I smiled in encouragement. Finally, he took both my hands and I helped him awkwardly onto the ice. "Don't let go." He asked softly.

"I won't." I answered. "Just follow my lead." I skated backwards as I coached Beau over a few laps. When he was getting his rhythm, I let go of one hand and we skated side by side slowly around the ice rink. "See, now you've got it." I praised.

He laughed, "Thanks. I can't believe I'm actually ice-skating. You are indeed a good teacher." He squeezed my hand in thanks.

"So why have you never skated before?" I found myself asking.

He considered this for a few moments then answered, "I think we were always just too busy. These ice-rinks pop up everywhere during one of our busiest seasons so even as a child, we really only had a break on Christmas Eve and that was spent at home."

"Did you always know you were going to follow in your father's footsteps?" I asked, with genuine curiosity about what made Beau Warner tick.

He nodded firmly, "Absolutely. As young as seven years old, I would rush to the hotel after school. I love that hotel, always have. I realised at a young age, that the people that worked there were good people needing to make ends meet. My father has a big heart, he gives anyone with a desire to do better in life an opportunity and if they worked hard, they were rewarded. Every staff member in our hotels is like family to us – as soon as they don the uniform, they are adopted into our family. And if they are ever in need, my father would do anything to help out."

"Oh that makes sense now. Nora told me that your Dad was consulting with a immigration lawyer to get her daughter and son here."

He nodded. "I am proud of that legacy and one that I intend to continue. But on a larger scale. My father has agreed on my plan for us to continue expanding around Europe."

"That's amazing. It's fantastic that you've always known what you wanted to do." Unlike me, who still had no clue.

We continued to skate hand in hand as I pondered on something Beau had said that niggled at me. He had said that every staff member was like family and they would do anything to help out. Was that what this ice-skating expedition was? An obligation? I tried to shake it off, but I was quickly realising I didn't want to be an obligation to Beau. I wanted to be his friend. I decided to be brave and broached the topic, however I wanted to keep the mood light so decided to go for a light and teasing tone, "So, I guess I'm like a sister to you, huh?"

He stopped skating suddenly, and the abrupt stop threw us both off-balance. A milli-second later, we were both on the ground and I landed squarely on top of him. "What the heck- why did you stop like that-?" I asked and I found myself face to face with Beau. Our eyes met and I could feel his heart rapidly beating even through the layers of clothing. My own heart echoed his.

"Why would you think that you're like a sister to me?" He whispered.

I needed to break this intimacy. I was starting to feel a tinge of attraction that I just could not and would not allow myself to acknowledge right now. It was the last thing I needed. I got up quickly, thankful for years of ice-skating that meant it was easy for me to maneuver myself on the ice. Once I was upright, I held out my hand to help Beau up as well. And as we dusted ourselves from the fall, I answered, again keeping my tone light hoping to ease the sudden tension that had built up between us, "You said that everyone that donned the uniform is like family to you… ergo, I'm like a sister."

He suddenly laughed and all tension melted away as his eyes gleamed with mischief. "Oh right. I see. No, you're not like a sister. You're more like that annoying perfect cousin that your mum keeps comparing you to. Look at you, you skate so well, I bet you do everything else well." Beau teased.

I laughed in response to his teasing but his comments struck me to the core. Oh how he couldn't be more farther from the truth. "Not even close. I am the hopeless one in my family!" Not wanting to have to elaborate, I changed the topic, "I'm starving. Let's see what's in the picnic basket."

A few minutes later, we had set up the rug in the marquee and we were relishing the warm pumpkin soup and fresh sourdough bread. We fell back into an easy conversation especially after we found that we had the same taste in music. We both listened to retro '90's R&B, hip hop and rap music. "No one writes music like this anymore." I commented as we listened to a Babyface hit on Beau's playlist.

"Right? I say that all the time." He raised a glass of sparkling water in agreement.

"My mum hates this music. Every time I played it loudly, as teenagers do, she would scream at me to turn it off." I laughed at the memory but stopped when it dawned on me that I would give anything now for my Mum to care enough to scream at me. Instead, I could probably play the baddest rap music in the flat and she wouldn't even budge out of her room. "I miss that." I admitted. "I wish my Mum would be present enough to care about anything. But she grieves so deeply."

Beau moved closer and then he reached out and squeezed my hand, comforting me once again.

"I saw a glimpse of her old self when we stripped off the ugliest wall paper in our flat and we painted the place together. I'm thinking of stripping off the hideous carpet and seeing what's underneath. Hopefully there are wooden floors hiding under there. That would be nice."

"You don't know this," Beau gleamed, "But you are actually talking to a handyman. I needed to learn how to be "handy" so I could be useful in the hotel as a teenager. I'll help you."

I leapt at this opportunity. Our flat needed a face-lift and here was a self-confessed handyman. There was no way I was going to let this slip by. "I would love that! Thank you! Thank you!" I hugged him in response and he just laughed and patted my back.

"Thank me after you've seen my work. I could be completely hopeless."

"I'm sure you'll be better than me, so that's good enough for me!" I laughed as I pulled out of the hug. "So when can we start?" I asked eagerly.

He smiled warmly, "Now, if you like? It's time to head home anyway so we can miss the traffic. Why don't I take you home and I can inspect what work needs doing." He started packing away the leftover soup and bread back into the picnic basket and I helped him pack up.

"Let me warn you now that you will be appalled when you see our dirty brown carpet. I think it was actually green at one stage."

"Green?" Beau asked incredulously. "Who chooses green carpet?"

"The same person that chose yellow and green wallpaper." I answered simply and laughed as Beau's eyes widened in shock.

"No they didn't."

"Yes they did. I could only hope that my grandparents were coerced into choosing those design elements or else I worry that I could be passing on colour-blindness in my DNA."

Beau laughed with gusto and at that moment, as I watched Beau, I realised that I didn't even think about Kane or about Olivia the entire time we were here.

# CHAPTER 9

eau parked his Alfa Romeo expertly in front of our building and within a few minutes we entered the flat. I felt a sense of unrest and instinctively I felt something wasn't quite right. It was only just after 3pm, a lot earlier than I would normally get home. The flat was quiet, but that wasn't unusual. Mum would be in bed either asleep or sadly, just staring into space. I looked around the flat and found nothing amiss. It was neat and tidy and everything was where they should be. "Mum, I'm home!" No response. Again, not unusual.

Beau took his coat and scarf off and he had the biggest smile on his face as he surveyed the place, "Ruth, you definitely need me! This place sure needs updating. Good job on the walls though. Looks good."

I laughed, trying to ignore my instinct that was telling me that something was wrong. "Thanks. And yes, I told you I need your help! Look at this carpet. Kitchen needs updating too, but we can tackle that later."

Beau nodded in agreement, then he asked, "Is your mother home? I'd love to meet her."

"Yes, she's home but she doesn't really leave her room. Let me check if she's up to it." I knocked on my mum's door and walked straight in.

The room was dark, the curtains were still down as always. I walked over to the window to draw up the curtains and let some light in. "Mum, we have a visitor and he wants to meet you…" I turned around and saw that she was asleep. "Mum-?" She didn't stir. "Mum!" That sense of dread filled my entire being and I knew there was something dreadfully wrong with Mum. I ran over to her and shook her shoulders to wake her up but she didn't respond. That's when I saw the empty bottle of painkillers on her bedside table. "Oh my god! Mum!" I screamed as I tried to check if she had a pulse.

Beau ran into the room and I heard him say, "Ruth, what happened?"

"Mum's overdosed on painkillers! She's not waking up! Beau, help me!" My fingers were shaking as I continued to try to feel for her pulse on her wrist but I couldn't feel a thing. Was she dead? I couldn't breathe. I was in a panic and I didn't know what to do.

"Call triple nine." Beau instructed and so I reached into my pocket for my phone as I watched him look for a pulse on her neck and wrist then within a second he was performing CPR on Mum. I started to cry. Had I lost Mum too? And it was my fault. I had failed her. I couldn't look after her well enough.

Emergency services answered immediately and between sobs I gave them a description of what was happening and my address. The person on the other line tried to calm me down but the only thing that was running through my head was that Mum was dead. I was now alone.

"Is your mother conscious?" The operator asked calmly.

"No. My friend is performing CPR." I sobbed. "I think she's dead."

Beau turned to me and he shook his head as he pumped my mum's chest, "Ruth, your mum is alive, she's got a weak pulse but I'm not going to let her die. Just tell them to come quickly."

Relief washed over me as I relayed what Beau had said to the operator.

It wasn't long at all before I heard the knock at our flat and the EMT came running into the room. They immediately took over and I rushed into Beau's arms for comfort as I continued to cry. I found myself saying a silent prayer, begging God not to let her die.

Mum was soon loaded onto a stretcher and as they moved to exit the room, one of the EMT turned to me and asked, "Did you want to accompany your mother to the hospital?" I nodded immediately and quickly moved out of Beau's arms as I mindlessly followed them into the ambulance.

Tears continued to flow as I sat silently in the ambulance, eyes glued onto my unconscious mother who was breathing through an oxygen mask. The EMT who was sitting across from me, a young man with red hair, freckles and friendly green eyes, reached out and patted me on the shoulder. "I'm sure your mother is going to be alright, thanks to your boyfriend. The CPR has kick started her heart and her pulse is stronger now. When we get to the hospital the doctors there will treat her."

His words gave me the hope I needed. I wiped my tears as I said a little prayer of thanks. I was thankful that I got home earlier than normal and I was thankful that Beau was with me.

We arrived at the hospital and there was a rush of activity as Mum was taken into ER. I went to follow her but was told I couldn't come into the ER, that I needed to stay in the waiting room. I felt alone, helpless and defeated as I found myself an empty chair in the crowded waiting room.

I fetched my phone from my jeans pocket as I remembered that I should let Olivia know what had happened. I called but she didn't pick up so I left a message but even as I was leaving the message I already knew that Olivia wouldn't come. Especially after what happened that morning.

I sighed as I made myself comfortable in the seat. The day's events replayed in my mind. When rains, it pours. I'd lost Dad and the boys, this morning I lost Olivia. Please God, don't let me lose Mum as well…

I continued to pray as minutes ticked by. There was nothing else to do but pray and wait.

I watched the various activities around me. A child came in crying, he was holding his arm and his parents looked like they were beside themselves. A broken arm, I suspected. The sliding door opened again and a man limped in and when I looked at his right foot I could see blood. A lot of blood. A woman was with him and she was screaming at him, it sounded like she was blaming him for the accident. Right behind them, a young man walked in carrying a woman's parka and bag. My heart stopped when I recognised Beau with my jacket and handbag. "Beau!" I stood up so he would see me.

He came over and handed me my stuff. "I thought you might need this. I locked up your flat as well and your keys are in your bag. I would have packed an overnighter, but I thought you might not appreciate me going through your stuff."

I was overwhelmed with gratefulness. I couldn't believe that such a generous and thoughtful man could exist. "Thank you, Beau. For this. But also for saving Mum's life-"

Beau interrupted, "I'm not a hero, Ruth. I did what anyone in that situation would do. How's your mum?"

"They're treating her now. They said they'll come and get me once they've stabilised her. I don't know how long that's going to be." I sat back down and Beau sat next to me.

"We'll wait together."

I turned my head to look at him, "You don't need to do that. I already took up your time all day today. I'm sure you're busy and have better things to do."

"What could be more important that being there for a friend when they need you?" And to make the point that he was staying, whether I wanted him to or not, he made himself more comfortable by stretching out his legs and then he proceeded to interlink his hands behind his head.

I smiled gratefully at him. "You are the best friend anyone could hope for."

"Close. The best friend would bring you coffee. I'll be right back." He stood up quickly and was gone in a flash. I found myself smiling as I watched Beau exit the building. He was a good man. We were virtually strangers, yet here he was being a good friend, not just once, but twice in one day!

He returned shortly with two large café lattes. "Here you go."

Gratefully, I took the coffee from him and took a sip. "Hmmm... thank you."

The anxious wait for news was made less strenuous with the light discussion that Beau led. We traded childhood stories and I even found myself smiling at some of his anecdotes.

"My family is close but we are also all workaholics. Dad actively oversees the London hotel. My mother runs a million committees and charities. I'm sure she works more hours than my father." He observed.

"Well my mum never really had a life outside her family. Our friends are, were-" I corrected myself "..all aristocrats and celebrities and my uncle made it his life's work to make sure my mum never felt like she belonged so I think she was never confident enough to go out there and prove him wrong. I guess that's why when we lost our family she doesn't feel like she has anything to live for." My voice croaked and tears welled in my eyes as I made myself acknowledge for the first time what Mum had done. This wasn't an accident. She had attempted to kill herself. She attempted suicide.

Beau took my hand and squeezed it. "I'm so sorry, Ruth."

"I've lost everyone, Beau. I can't lose her too." He was about to take me into his arms when we heard my name being called out. We both stood up quickly and rushed towards the doctor who was calling my name.

"Ruth, I'm Doctor Ku. I treated your mother and she's going to be okay. She's stable. She regained consciousness a couple of hours ago, which is a great sign. Although she's asleep now, she's had a big day and she's exhausted, but I can take you to see her if you wish." I nodded and instantly found myself taking Beau's hand. I wanted him to come with me. I guess I didn't want to have to face this alone.

We were ushered into a ward where most beds had their privacy curtains open. I saw my mum immediately and without waiting for Doctor Ku, I led Beau towards Mum's bed.

She looked frail. Even more than she ever had before. I started to cry again, as I re-lived the nightmare of finding her unconscious and the fact that I almost lost her. I was grateful for Beau's presence as I leaned on him for support.

A nurse organised a couple of chairs to be placed by Mum's bed and Beau led me there and sat me down. Doctor Ku knelt down in front of me and smiled empathetically, "She should wake up in a few hours. I'm happy for you to stay here until then or you can head home and come back in the morning."

It was getting late but I wanted to stay. I wanted to be there when she awoke. "I want to stay."

"Alright. We are going to move her out of ER when she wakes, so you can stay here until then."

Beau and I waited for Mum to wake up. We sat together and we talked while we waited. We talked about inconsequential things like music, food, books and about the celebrities we knew or have encountered.

When my stomach growled, Beau fetched us dinner. At 11pm, Mum still hadn't woken up but the nurse assured me that everything was fine.

"Are you sure you don't want to go home?" I asked Beau, giving him an out.

Beau answered quickly, "No. I'm fine here. Besides, you were just about to tell me your most embarrassing moments from your childhood. I certainly don't want to miss that."

I was relieved he wanted to stay. Truth be told, I didn't want him to leave. I appreciated having him here with me. I appreciated the fact that I didn't have to do this on my own.

I heard coughing and someone calling my name and it was only then that I realised I had fallen asleep. I opened my eyes and instantly became fully aware that I slept in Beau's arms. He was still asleep, his head was bent back and my head was resting on his chest as his arms kept me, and the light blue cotton blanket, in place. I turned my head and saw that Mum was also just waking up.

The noise must had also woken up Beau. I could feel him raising his head and so I turned my head to look at him and our eyes met. He smiled at me, "Your mother's awake."

I nodded and smiled back as I quickly got up.

"Mum!" I hugged her immediately and she hugged me back.

We both looked up when we felt Beau standing behind me. "Who's this?" Mum queried. Her voice was soft and scratchy.

"Mum, this is my friend, Beau. He saved your life."

Mum looked up at Beau and tears rolled down her cheeks. "Thank you." She said simply yet those words were filled with emotion.

Beau smiled warmly in response. "I was glad I was there to help. Now I think I should leave so you can be alone." He turned to me and he took my hand, "You don't need to go to work. It's 4 a.m. now and I'm sure you'll need your rest. Take as long as you need." I nodded gratefully and he turned and walked away.

"He's a nice young man." Mum said when he was out of sight.

"Just a friend, Mum. A friend that happened to be there when… Oh Mum, why did you do it?" I sobbed.

"I'm tired, Ruth. Besides, I'm a burden to you. You're better off without me. If I'm not here, you can go back to your old life." Mum's tears flowed and I held on to her tight, knowing that I had nearly lost her and so grateful that she was there, that she was alive for me to hold.

"I don't need my old life back, Mum. I need you. I can't lose you too. Please Mum, don't do that again." I cried out.

"Oh Ruth. I'm sorry to be putting you through this. I'm so sorry." Mum's voice was weak but I heard genuine remorse.

The next few hours flew by as Mum was moved from the ER to a two-bed recovery room. We were thankful when Mum was allocated the bed by the window. It made the room feel less claustrophobic! The doctors and nurses continued her treatment and throughout this, I stayed. I couldn't make myself go home, I was too scared that something would happen while I was away.

Later that day, I was sitting with Mum while she slept when an Amazonian of a woman approached us. She looked to be in her fifties, tall and imposing, with dark hair and piercing blue eyes. If Wonder Woman was in her fifties, this was exactly how she would look. But when she spoke she had the gentlest voice I had ever heard. "I'm Dr. Lydia Campbell, you must be Ruth." She sat down next to me and I immediately liked her. I was instantly comfortable with her. There was something about her that calmed me, that gave me hope.

"Yes, I'm Ruth." I nodded in acknowledgment.

"Dr. Ku called me. I'm a psychologist and I'm here to help your mum." With those gentle words, I started to cry, but this time I cried because I felt as if a load was lifted off my shoulders. There was someone here to help Mum. I wasn't alone. As I stared at Dr. Campbell, a sense of peace settled over me. I knew deep within my heart that everything was going to be okay.

# CHAPTER 10

*A* sound startled me out of my light sleep. The bed next to my mum's was vacated last night and the nurse on night shift was kind enough to offer it to me so I could stay. I quickly sat up and saw that Dr. Campbell had walked in and had started a conversation with Mum. They both looked at me and they both smiled.

"Good morning sleepy-head." It was how Mum greeted me every morning when I was little. I couldn't help but feel nostalgic as I remembered those good old days and I felt hope that maybe my mum was getting back to her old self.

"'Morning Mum, good morning Dr. Campbell." I replied as I walked over to give Mum a kiss on the cheek, just like I used to when I was little.

Dr. Campbell nodded her head in acknowledgement, the smile still dominating her kind face. "Good morning to you too, Ruth. I've come for your mum's first session. I'm pleased that we have the room to ourselves so we can actually hold the session here. Now, I need forty-five minutes with your mum, so I suggest that you take the opportunity to get yourself some breakfast, have some coffee and we can then chat after the session. Do you mind?"

"Not at all." I quickly grabbed my bag and walked out. The sooner my mum started therapy the sooner she would get better.

I couldn't have taken more than five steps when I heard Nora calling me. "Ruth, Ruth! There you are!" I was immediately enveloped into her arms and I bent down to return her hug. And it suddenly occurred to me that I had been too busy worrying about Mum that I had completely forgotten to let Nora know what had happened! Thankfully, it looked like Beau had done that job for me. Of course I felt guilty not being the one to tell Nora myself. She'd been so good to me.

Before I could apologise, the ever-effervescent Nora exclaimed loudly, "My poor baby! Oh my Lord, you have been through so much already and now this..."

"Mum's going to be okay." I whispered, embarrassed as I could see everyone around the nurse's station staring at us.

"Of course she is! Your Mum is going to get through this! In the meantime, I got our superintendent to open your flat so I can grab some clothes for you and your mum, some toiletries and other things I thought you might need. Beau said you didn't have time to get supplies."

Nora was such a gem! Grateful, I hugged her tighter. "Thank you Nora. I don't know what I'd do without you. Let me shout you breakfast as a thank you." I took the overnight bag from her and together we walked to the hospital cafeteria.

Over filtered coffee and croissants, I gave her an update on Mum's condition. Nora held my hand tightly, "Ruth, take as long as you need. Did I tell you about Lilli? You know the girl that left us in a lurch when she eloped with her French lover? Well she's come crawling back. He ended up having another family and she found out and left him. So she's back and I felt sorry for her so I've hired her back. So don't worry about us, we're okay."

I shook my head. "No, I'll be back tomorrow. Mum is recovering well."

"Focus on helping your mum recover and your job will be waiting for you when you're ready." Nora insisted.

"I'll be back tomorrow. Mum's in good hands here and she's through the worse. I'll see you tomorrow." I was conscious that I'd been away from work too often. They'd been too kind already and I didn't want to take advantage.

"Okay. If that's the way you want it. I support you either way."

I couldn't find the words to express how grateful I was to Nora. 'Thank you' didn't feel enough. Nevertheless, I whispered my thanks and I wiped the tears that welled in my eyes as I got up and hugged her.

Dr. Campbell was waiting for me outside Mum's hospital room. As I walked over, she motioned me over to the set of chairs by the nurse's station. "How's Mum?" I asked immediately.

"Ruth, your mum is suffering from depression. From my conversation with her today, it's very likely that she's been suffering from a mild case of depression for years however the loss of your father and brothers has triggered a severe depression."

Depression. A sense of clarity washed over me as I thought back to my mum's behaviour the last few months and even the last few years. She had depression. How could I have not realised that before? Because if I had known, maybe I would have pushed her to see a psychologist sooner and it wouldn't have gotten this bad. I stayed with her because I wanted to help her. Yet I wasn't smart enough to pick up on the fact that she needed help. Yet again, I had failed.

As if Dr. Campbell could read my mind, "It's not your fault, Ruth. Even if you had known, it's likely your mum wouldn't have admitted it and she wouldn't have willingly sought help. Okay? I want you to know two important things. The first is that depression is common. 1 in 4 people suffer from depression here in the UK. The second thing I want you to know is that it is an illness. And just like any illness, we will put a treatment plan in place for your Mum and she will recover. I get a sense from your mum that she wants to get better, she just doesn't know how. I will help her. There is hope, Ruth. It will be a hard battle for your mum, but she can get better. Physically, she is recovering well, and Dr. Ku is happy to discharge your mum at the end of the week. They just want to continue to monitor her recovery until then. However at this stage I am concerned for her mental health so once she is released from here I recommend that your mum be moved to the hospital in Westminster that I volunteer at. They have a very good psychiatric ward there. We need your mum to stay there until I am satisfied that she is no longer a danger to herself. I personally will treat her there. Does that work for you?"

I nodded without hesitation. I would agree to anything that would help Mum recover. "Of course." I answered automatically.

"Good. I'll be back tomorrow, same time, to continue her treatment."

"Thank you." Again, those sentiments didn't feel like it was enough to express my gratitude. The English language really should have something that conveyed gratitude that exceeded a mere 'thank you.' Those words were uttered so thoughtlessly when someone opened the door for us, or when a stranger picked up something we dropped. Yet the level of care I was experiencing right now from Dr. Campbell, from Nora and from Beau was well beyond what I could ever expect, yet there was only one way to say 'thank you'. I repeated my thanks, hoping that by saying it again it helped to express the immense gratitude I felt.

Mum was looking out the window when I walked in. "It's going to snow." She observed without looking at me.

"Looks like it might." I agreed, accepting the small talk.

"Did you see Dr. Campbell on your way in?" Mum turned to me and watched as I took the seat by her bed.

I nodded. I didn't know what to say. I didn't know what I should say. I didn't know what I could say. Dr. Campbell was right. Depression was common. I had friends that had been popping anti-depressants pretty much their whole lives and I even had a couple of friends who had tried to off themselves as early as thirteen years old. Yet I realised that none of those experiences prepared me for this. I just didn't know what to say to my own mother who was suffering from severe depression. I was too worried I would say the wrong thing and I would make her worse.

After a few minutes of silence, it was Mum that spoke first. "I loved your dad. I admit, it was his family title and money that attracted me at first. I was with someone else when I met your Dad. But boy he was charming. I couldn't help myself. I was working as a receptionist in a tax agent's office and he walked in with his friend. We flirted. He came back the next day. And every day for a whole week until I agreed to go on a date. My boss told me who he was and I agreed on a date. The thing is, I fell in love with your Dad after I got to know him. When I walked down the aisle it was because I loved him, not because of his father's title or his money. I thought we were going to grow old together. I thought I was going to watch Kyle graduate, start his own practice, get married, have children. And Mark... when I found out I was pregnant with another child when we had given up hope of having any more children, I was so happy, he was my precious baby. I wanted to see him become a man." Mum closed her eyes and took a deep breath, "Since they were taken from me, I've had this pain, this piercing pain in my chest. I've cried and cried and suddenly I've stopped feeling any emotions. All I'm left with is this pain in my chest. It doesn't stop. I couldn't bear the pain anymore. I just wanted it to stop. I could only think of one way of stopping the pain.

And I figured I'd be doing you a favour, Ruth, because I'll be setting you free."

Her confession tore me inside. I ran to Mum and I hugged her tight. "We'll get through this together, Mum. You're going to get better."

Mum didn't respond. Instead she took my hand, squeezed it and said simply, "I'm so tired. So, so tired." She settled herself into the bed and closed her eyes.

While Mum was asleep, I took the opportunity to charge my phone (Nora thought of everything!). My phone had been dead since last night and I wondered, even hoped, that Olivia had messaged back.

I took a shower while I waited for my phone to power up, and as soon as I finished I checked my phone. Only one text message. And it wasn't from Olivia, rather it was from Beau sent a couple of hours ago.

"How's your mum? How are you?" The message said.

I was touched by Beau's thoughtfulness. I messaged back, "Sorry, phone was dead. Just got your message. Mum ok but need to move to psych ward when released here. I'm ok."

Immediately, Beau messaged back, "Do you want company?"

He really was such a sweetheart. But I didn't want him to have to drop everything to be with me. That was asking a lot from someone whom I just met. So I replied, "Thank you but I'm ok here. I'll see you at work tomorrow anyway." I added a smiley emoji to emphasise that I was really fine.

He messaged back, "Alright. We can also get started on your flat tomorrow after work, if you like?"

I smiled as I read Beau's message. "Sure! Would love that!" It would be fantastic if we could surprise Mum with new floors for her homecoming! A rush of excitement flowed through me, grateful for Beau's friendship.

# CHAPTER 11

traight after my shift the next day, I headed to the hospital to visit Mum. The plan was that I would stay there for a couple of hours and then Beau would pick me up to take me home so we could get started on the floors. Mum was feeling slightly better that day and she attributed that to Dr. Campbell. I was glad to hear that therapy was helping and hope continued to grow within me. Dr. Ku was even hopeful that she could be transferred to the psychiatric ward even as early as tomorrow.

At 6pm, I hopped into Beau's Alfa Romeo and the smell of grilled prawns made me lick my lips. The smell was mouth-watering! "Oh my, what's that smell?"

Beau laughed, "I know, my stomach's been rumbling throughout the drive here because of that smell. It's our dinner, compliments of Chef Leon. He said you forgot to pick up your dinner today."

"You know about that? Chef Leon kindly offered to give us leftovers from the kitchen. I hope you don't mind?" I worried that Chef Leon might get in trouble because surely it wasn't a standard practice to give out food to the hotel staff?

But Beau merely shrugged, "That's fine. What he does in his kitchen is his business. I wouldn't dare tell him what to do. We wouldn't want to anger our star head chef!" He laughed and changed the subject by asking about Mum. Gratefully, I took the bait and told him the good news that she might be released earlier.

We were both starving by the time we walked into the flat so I immediately went about re-heating the prawns, mashed potatoes and roasted asparagus that came with it. Meanwhile, Beau downed his toolbox by the door and set the table for two.

Within a few minutes we were tucking into our dinner. "This is delicious." I sighed with pleasure.

Beau smiled warmly at me and he nodded his agreement. "We can actually take our time eating dinner, we don't have much to do tonight. The first thing we need to do is check what's under the carpet and our next course of action is dependent on what we find."

"Dear Lord, please let there be floorboards under that eyesore!" I put my hands together in a gesture of prayer.

"That would definitely be best case scenario. Either way, we won't rip the entire carpet out until we're ready. It will get too cold in here, otherwise. Depending on what we see under the carpet, tonight will be all about planning. Are you good with that?"

"I'm completely at your mercy Mr. DIY!" I said lightheartedly, hiding the depth of gratitude and overwhelming relief I felt that he was here with me, being a true friend.

He laughed and the conversation continued as Beau shared some of his DIY disasters and some of them were so disastrous we both laughed until our bellies ached. Especially about the time Beau admitted to gluing his fingers together. "But I've learnt from my mistakes, so you can trust me. I really do know what I'm doing now!" He added as I continued to laugh.

"Okay then. Prove it. Let's get started!" I exclaimed eagerly as I cleared the plates away.

A few minutes later, Beau knelt at the corner of the lounge room and I stood eagerly behind him. "Moment of truth." He stated as he ripped the corner of the carpet out with a utility knife. We spied the wooden floorboards at the same time.

I was so excited to see it. I jumped up and down, "Yes! Yes! Yes! Floorboards!" I exclaimed in delight and found myself hugging Beau when he stood up to face me.

He was laughing at my excitement and he hugged me back. It only lasted a second as Beau then picked up his notebook and pen. "Alright, let's make a list of what we need and I'll go buy the supplies tomorrow while you're visiting your Mum."

"Okay, but remember I'm on a budget." I warned as we sat down on the couch. We spent the next half hour planning and making lists. When Beau left that night, I surveyed the flat as I pictured what the place would look like with floorboards. For the first time in a very long time, I slept with a smile on my face.

The next evening, Beau and I were wearing coveralls, masks and goggles. I found myself laughing at how ridiculous I looked, especially since the coveralls were way too big for me. I was in a great mood. Mum was transferred to the psychiatric ward in Westminster, which meant that physically she had recovered well and now we could focus on her mental health.

I lowered the mask and continued to laugh as I pictured Eve's face if she ever caught me wearing this outfit, "If my old friends could see me now, they would just die. I'm not sure what they would have been more shocked to see me in – my housekeeping uniform or this ensemble."

"I think you look cute in both." He said teasingly, as he too lowered his mask and adjusted his goggles. Then under his breath I heard him whisper, "You'd look cute in anything."

I wasn't sure whether I was meant to hear that comment but I did and I found myself blushing despite the fact that I'd heard those very words all my life. Somehow, it meant more coming from Beau.

A second later though, my insecurities reared its ugly head. I started to wonder why Beau was happy to give up his spare time to help me out. Was he expecting more than friendship? Did he have an ulterior motive? Why would someone as amazing as Beau want to spend his time with me? I needed to know. So I asked, "Beau, why are you being so nice to me? Why are you giving up your evenings to help me?"

There was no hesitation with his answer. He simply said, "Because we're friends. Don't you go out of your way to help your friends?" I was taken aback. He was right. Of course I went out of my way to help my friends. In fact, I was always the one my friends turned to when they needed someone to talk to. Every time Eve fought with her father or any of her stepmothers, I dropped everything to be with her. I cheered her up and counselled her on what to do. It was like that with all my friends. It made me happy to help.

Gratefully, I smiled at Beau. "What did I do to deserve your friendship?"

Beau smiled back, "You didn't have to do anything. It's freely given. Now... we should get started. First thing's first, we need to move the furniture..." We packed the sofa and other furniture into Mum's room and went about ripping the carpet starting from one corner of the lounge room.

We settled into a comfortable routine. During day I went to work, in the evenings I visited Mum in Westminster (an easier commute from

Mayfair), then Beau picked me up to take me back to the flat where we ate dinner supplied by Chef Leon, followed by a couple of hours work on the floors. During my days off, I spent the extra time with Mum, who was making a steady progress, according to Dr. Campbell.

In just over two weeks, the floors to the lounge room and bedrooms were done. On top of that, we stripped the lino flooring in the kitchen that also revealed wooden floorboards underneath so we brought that to life as well. As Beau and I moved the final furniture back to its place, my phone started to ring. It was Dr. Campbell. I answered it immediately; worried that something might have happened to my mum.

"Hello?" I answered.

"Hi Ruth. It's Dr. Campbell here. No need to worry. I call bearing good news. I came by to see your mum this evening and I'm fully satisfied that she is no longer an immediate harm to herself so I plan to release her tomorrow."

It was the news I had been waiting to hear. "That's amazing! Thank you, Dr. Campbell." Tomorrow was my birthday and this news was the best birthday present I could ever hope for.

"Your mum did the heavy lifting. Credit goes to her. You should be very proud of your mum. Come by after work tomorrow and the release papers should be ready by then."

We said our farewell and without realising it, I was doing a happy dance and Beau watched me in amusement. "Good news, obviously?"

"The best news! Mum's coming home tomorrow. How perfect is that timing?"

"That is the best news! I am so pleased!" Beau took me in his arms, picked me up and spun me around. And while in his arms, I had to admit that I more than liked these little moments with him. "I'll take you to pick up your mum so you don't have to take a cab home." I thanked Beau, grateful for his thoughtfulness.

The flat looked great. It looked fresh. And with the expensive furniture and furnishings we brought with us from our townhouse, the place actually could be mistaken for a showroom. The only thing the place needed were new kitchen appliances and a complete renovation of the bathroom – all out of reach at the moment, given our financial situation. Setting that aside, I was extremely happy with the way the floorboards made the place look modern and feel so much more habitable. Mum surveyed the apartment and as she did her smile grew wide. "I've never seen this place look this good. You both did this?"

"Yes we did, Mum! Do you love it?" I boasted, putting my arm around my mum.

"I do, indeed. I'm very proud of you. Thank you, Ruth. For everything." She kissed me on the cheek and suddenly we heard the unmistakable 'pop' of a champagne bottle opening.

There in the kitchen was Beau pouring the bubbles into champagne glasses. Beside the glasses was a luscious-looking chocolate cake with candles all lit up. He started singing "Happy Birthday to you…" and my Mum joined in as we walked towards Beau at the kitchen counter.

I was shocked. Completely surprised. I hadn't planned to celebrate my birthday at all! I turned eighteen today but I didn't think it was as important as Mum's homecoming. Incredulous and incredibly happy that someone had put so much effort for me, I paused to make a wish – that Mum would continue to get better – then I blew out the candles.

Mum was cheering, like she always did whenever we blew out the candles on our birthdays.

Beau handed Mum and I a glass of champagne each, and he proposed a toast, "To Ruth, happy birthday! We are more the richer for having you in our lives. And to Naomi, welcome home." We clinked our glasses and happily sipped the bubbles.

"So how did you know it was my birthday?" I asked Beau a few minutes later.

"Nora, of course. She should be here soon with dinner. So we have to wait until after dinner before we have the cake. I just wanted to surprise you first." He winked cheekily, obviously pleased that he managed to pull off the surprise.

Sure enough, within half an hour, Nora walked in carrying a feast, courtesy of Chef Leon.

The four of us sat down for dinner and the conversation was easy and it was fun. As I looked around the table, laughing at one of Nora's funny stories about a hotel customer, I was overwhelmed with joy. Finally, after months of darkness, light was starting to seep through the cracks.

# CHAPTER 12

r. Campbell's office looked and felt like a haven. As Nora and I sat there, waiting for Mum's appointment to finish, I felt immediately at ease. The place didn't feel like a clinic, it felt like home. The warm tones, large brown leather couches, cozy fireplace and the receptionist's grand mahogany desk welcomed us as if it was a home office. It reminded me of Dad's library in our townhouse. I loved that room. I loved the times I spent there with Dad when I was a child. It was there that he taught me how to play chess and it was where he read me poems by Donne, Blake, Yeats and Wordsworth. I looked over at the large matching mahogany bookshelf next to the fireplace. It was full of books, some looked to be medical books but I spied some English literature amongst them. The same types of books my dad loved reading. Surprisingly, the reminders of Dad didn't bring pain, instead it made me feel like he was with me. It was comforting.

Nora, being Nora, couldn't sit still. A few minutes later, she stood up and walked over to the friendly receptionist, a brunette in her mid-twenties, trendy black-rimmed glasses and a big smile. "Can I help you?" She asked.

"Kat, right? Have you worked here long?" I smiled at Nora's question. She was the best at starting small talk.

"Just over two years. It's great here. Dr. Campbell is fantastic." Kat cooed.

But of course, Nora wasn't finished with her. "Have you got boyfriend?" My smile widened at Nora's boldness. She wasn't shy to go straight to the personal questions!

"I do. Tim and I have been together for three years now. He's an Aussie. He's so lovely-"

Kat was saved from having to answer any more personal questions when the door to Dr. Campbell's office opened and both Mum and the doctor walked out together.

I stood up, my eyes immediately focusing on Mum, looking for any signs of how she was feeling. She looked like she had been crying however I could see peace in her facial expression and in her body language. I let out a long breath that I didn't know I was holding.

Dr. Campbell walked over to me and patted my left upper arm, "Ruth, your mum is doing very well. No need to worry. Now I hear that Christmas shopping is next on the agenda for you today?"

I nodded. "Yes. It's only a week before Christmas so we've left it very late! It's likely to be chaos out there."

Mum walked over to join the conversation. "We're going to have to split up. You can't see what I'm buying you for Christmas."

"No problem!" Nora immediately went on solution-mode. "Naomi, why don't you and I go shopping together? We can also buy new clothes, have some afternoon tea… We can make a day of it! We can give Ruth a break, a day all to herself."

Mum smiled. The smile reached her eyes. I hadn't seen that in a long time. "Yes! Nora, that is a brilliant idea. No arguments, Ruth, you deserve this. You haven't had a day to yourself in a very long time."

Dr. Campbell clapped her hands once, signaling finality. "Well that's it then. Ruth, you have the day to yourself." Then she whispered to me, "I would encourage your mum's friendship with Nora. She needs that. This is a good idea. Nora will make sure she's okay."

I nodded and echoed Dr. Campbell's conclusion. "Well that's it then. I am having the day to myself! Enjoy yourselves!" Dr. Campbell was right, of course. Mum needed a friend and who better than Nora? I had absolute trust in Nora to look after my mum. Besides, she was fun, caring and hilarious – exactly the type of person my mum needed in her life.

After a second of goodbyes, I found myself alone outside Dr. Campbell's building, not knowing what to do with myself. However I didn't have to worry about having to make a decision because my phone buzzed shortly with a message from Beau, "Need a favour. We are down a player for bowling. Are you free? Please?"

Bowling? I hadn't played since I was in my tweens but after everything Beau had done for me, I couldn't turn down a favour. "Of course. When and where?"

Beau responded quickly, "Now? Brick Lane. I can come and pick you up."

I wasn't too far so I responded. "No need. I'll meet you there in twenty minutes."

As soon as I walked in, I spotted Beau and his friends immediately. They were hard to miss in their bright red and blue bowling shirts. The place was small, with only a few lanes but it was teeming with people and energy.

Beau spotted me. I could see him walking over with a huge smile on his beautiful face. "Hi!"

"Hi." I smiled back.

"Thank you for coming. You are a lifesaver. The comp is starting in half an hour and we are a player down."

"Wait – you never said anything about a competition!" I started getting nervous, not wanting to let Beau and his friends down. "I haven't played since I was eleven."

Beau took my gloved hand and he started leading me towards the group. "Don't worry, it's not a serious comp. We just didn't want to be booted off because we didn't have enough players. He turned and our eyes met, "Let's just have fun!".

"Alright." I answered with a smile but the nervousness remained firmly in place.

We stopped at lane 3 and Beau made quick introductions. "Ruth, meet The Oxford Pinheads! Colin, Patricia (you can call her Pat) and Saskia. Mark's home sick with the 'flu and he's usually our anchor, so we're down our best player. Team, meet Ruth, our lifesaver."

Colin, Pat and Saskia immediately went in for a group hug. "Thank you, Ruth!" They all looked like they were there to have fun. I suddenly felt at ease. Relieved.

Colin, who was tall, lanky and quite attractive walked over to his bag and pulled out a matching bowling shirt. "Ruth, this will be way too big for you, but I'm sure you can make it work."

Beau took the shirt while I took off my gloves, scarf and jacket. He then helped me put on the bowling shirt over my long sleeved shirt. It went down pass my knees. Beau laughed, "You look like a child playing dress ups." I laughed too and immediately went about making myself presentable. I left the buttons undone at the front and knotted the shirt across my stomach. Fortunately, I was wearing my black long sleeved shirt underneath and black leather pants so at least the colours were not clashing!

I heard Beau breathe in deeply. "Wow, you really can make anything look attractive, even a baggy bowling shirt. "

I found myself blushing. My heart was beating fast again, but this time it wasn't from the nerves.

Pat came over, "Love what you've done with Mark's shirt. Come on, let's get you your shoes." She linked her arm with mine as she led me away. "You are gorgeous. I wish I can be the same size as you. I am constantly on a diet but nothing works." Pat was of similar height to me and yes, she was a few sizes bigger but she was gorgeous herself.

"You're beautiful, Pat. You don't need to lose weight. What diet were you on anyway?"

Pat shrugged and smiled, "The tomorrow diet."

I frowned. My friends and I were always in the know when it came to diet fads yet I've never heard of it. "What is that?" I asked.

"It's one where I eat as much as I want today and say to myself, 'Diet starts tomorrow!'" We laughed together and I knew instantly that we were going to be friends.

As we waited in line, we continued our chat. "So you're all obviously Beau's friends from university?"

Pat nodded. "Yeah. He, Mark and Colin are good friends and so when I started going out with Colin last year, we started hanging out. Saskia and Beau have been friends since high school but it wasn't until Oxford that they started hanging out. Mark and Saskia are now an item. They've been together about a month now."

I looked behind me where Saskia and Beau were chatting, they had their heads close to each other as they laughed at something Beau had said. I suddenly felt a pang of jealousy. I brushed it aside. I had no right to feel jealous. Pat put her arm around my shoulder and winked, "Don't worry. There was never anything between Saskia and Beau. They are more like siblings. Beau never showed any interest in relationships. We all thought he was married to his hotels. And he was until you came along."

Her words had an extraordinary effect on me. I wanted to sing out loud with happiness! Yet at the same time, I didn't want to admit that there was anything between us. Because Beau deserved better than someone like me. I was an ex-party girl with no future. I had nothing to offer him. Tamping down any feelings of happiness, of hope, I shook my head in denial, "We're just friends."

Pat smiled knowingly, "Sure you are." By that time though, we were at the front of the line and so I gratefully took the reprieve and ordered my bowling shoes.

There were six teams competing. The two lowest scoring teams in each round would be knocked out and the top two scoring teams at the end of Round 2 would vie for the championship trophy. By the time the competition kicked off, cocktails were flowing and so were American hotdogs and pizzas. As Colin took the lane to bowl, Saskia handed me over a margarita, "I know you said you were sticking to water, but I'm sure one won't hurt." She smiled warmly.

"Thank you. I just want to make sure I don't let you all down."

Saskia sat next me, "Didn't Beau explain that it's just a friendly comp? None of us are pros. You'll be fine. Besides, if it was all about winning, Beau would have asked his neighbour, Joe, he's known to play perfect games. But he didn't. So just go out there and have fun!"

I didn't have time to digest Saskia's revelation because Beau was calling my name. It was my turn.

I picked up the bright purple ball I had pre-selected and walked over to bowl. I took a deep breath and I bowled. Amazingly, I watched the bowl knock over every single pin. It was a strike.

I turned around with an incredulous expression and saw that my whole team was on their feet cheering for me. Beau walked over to me with a huge smile, "You really hadn't played since you were a kid?" I nodded, pleased with myself. "I knew you'd be a natural. You're good at anything you put your mind to."

Not wanting to set high expectations I might not be able to deliver, I answered, "Maybe it was just beginner's luck?"

It wasn't. I found myself easily able to bowl a strike or a spare. I kept up with Beau's scores. By the end of two rounds, our team was through to the finals.

The competition was tough. The other team was playing close to a perfect game. I was down to my final frame and I needed a strike to keep our team in the game. As I walked up, I could hear the whole place chanting my name, "Ruth, Ruth, Ruth…" It was a lot of pressure, but I found that I was able to keep my cool. And I was actually having a lot of fun!

I drowned the noise and focused on what I had to do. I bowled. And it was like it was played in slow motion as I watched the ball make its way along the alley, skirting close to the gutter then curving its way closer to the middle where it then knocked one pin, then two until all the pins laid scattered. The place erupted with joy. I turned around to face the crowd, and I did a little victory jig.

Beau came running to me and he took me into his arms and swung me around and round. I was laughing when he put me down. He kept me in his arms as he praised, "That was amazing!" He then kissed my forehead.

I suddenly couldn't breathe as my heart felt like it was pounding out of my chest. I was so aware of Beau… handsome, intelligent and the nicest person I knew. I was in his arms and it felt good. It felt right. It was at that moment that I knew… I was falling in love with Beau.

Then of course, the logical side of my brain brought me back to reality. He was too good for me. Besides, we were just friends. Beau never said or alluded to being more than that. I was headed for a broken heart and I knew that it wasn't something I could recover from very quickly. I needed to put a stop to this.

Straightening up, I moved away from his embrace and I put on an expression that I hoped looked nonchalant, "Thanks!" I then turned to the rest of the team who came over for a team hug.

We ended up winning the competition so the team stuck around for celebratory cocktails. The venue had a local band playing to liven up the mood, not that the group needed it. The chatter was a lot of fun. Especially coming from Pat who was the resident comedian. She teased everyone mercilessly, no one was exempted.

Soon, Pat zeroed in on Beau, "This band is terrible. Beau you should get up there and takeover." She teased.

"No way." Beau answered back quickly, his face going red.

I turned to him in surprise, "You play?" Realising just how little I really knew of Beau.

"Terribly. My mother made me take guitar lessons when I was a kid. These guys just like to tease."

Pat decided to change the topic then and within seconds she had the entire group in stitches.

It was late by the time we called it a night. I was relieved when I saw that Beau was also driving Saskia home and since they lived closer to each other, I would be first to be dropped off. I really didn't want to be alone with him just yet, not when my newfound feelings for him were still quite raw. I wasn't sure how accomplished I was as an actor and until

I was able to control it, it wasn't a good idea to have any time alone with Beau. So, when he stopped his Alfa in front of my building, I didn't even give him an opportunity to get out and walk me to my door. I jumped out and ran. I heard him get out and call my name, but I didn't stop. I kept running until I was inside the flat.

# CHAPTER 13

We survived our first Christmas without Dad and the boys. And without Olivia. Christmas was always a huge deal for our family. We could do whatever we wanted for New Year's Eve, but Mum and Dad insisted that Christmas was spent with family. Yet despite the painful reminders of happy Christmases spent together as a large family, Mum and I got through it. Together. We closeted ourselves within our flat and we took solace in each other's company. We didn't decorate the flat with Christmas decorations. We both weren't ready for that. However we did cook up a nice pork roast on Christmas Eve and had a relaxing night talking about everything but Christmas memories. That topic was avoided all together.

Our decision to face the festive season as hermits was also a good excuse to distance myself from Beau. He had invited me over for dinner after work a few times during the week and I had the ready excuse that Mum needed me. Thankfully, it wasn't truly a lie. There were moments when it was obvious that Mum struggled. Truthfully, I struggled myself. However I could see how Mum's sessions with Dr. Campbell was helping her manage her depression. She had tools she utilised when she needed it. I was in awe of how far Mum had come in just over a month. Yes, she still wasn't her old self, but she was now able to engage with the world around her again and our relationship was deepening because of it. We actually enjoyed the nights spent quietly in each other's company.

So when the thirty-first of December came, I expected another quiet night with Mum, that was until I got a text message from her while I was sitting in The Warner's staff common room during my lunch break, "Ruth, I hope you don't mind, Nora is taking me to her friend's party tonight. You should also go out with friends. Love Mum." For the first time in my entire life, I was going to be alone for New Year's Eve. Surprisingly enough, a quiet night at home by myself didn't sound too bad.

"What are you doing tonight?" One of the women I was sitting with asked.

"Well, I was going to spend it with my mum but that message was just from her saying she's got other plans." I smiled and shrugged. "It will just be a quiet one for me."

"You must come out with us, then! We're hitting the clubs tonight."

It was the last thing I wanted to do. Somehow, without realising it, that part of me - the party girl - was buried along with Dad, Kyle and Mark. I was spared from having to reply by a tall presence by the doorway. It was Beau.

"There you are." He walked in and took the seat next to me. The three ladies I was sitting with suddenly stood up and excused themselves. "Please, stay." Beau asked them but it was too late, they were already bolting from the common room.

I couldn't help but laugh, "Wow, you do know how to scare the girls." I joked.

But his answer was serious as he searched my face, "Is that why you're avoiding me? Have I scared you?"

I could feel my face redden as the truth of his words hit me. I wasn't scared of him but I was scared of my feelings for him. Of course, I only had one way of replying to his question… denial. "No of course not, it was a tough time for Mum so I needed to be with her."

"I absolutely understand that. But I also know it was a tough time for you as well. I wanted to be there for you like you were there for your Mum. We're friends, right?"

His thoughtfulness warmed my heart. I really didn't want to lose him as a friend. Real friends were so hard to come by. I just needed to get over my feelings for him. Friendship, that was all it could ever be. That was all I wanted it to be. "Yes, absolutely. Of course we're still friends."

"Great. Well, friend, come to my family's New Year's Eve Party tonight at my parents' house in Buckinghamshire. Colin and crew will be there so it will be a lot of fun."

I hated to admit it, but after a week of running away, my resolve was weakening. I really, really wanted to go so I found myself nodding, while in my head I chanted, "I'm strong. I'm in control of my feelings…"

By eight thirty that night, I was dressed in a long Dolce & Gabbana black sheer tulle dress with red floral embroidery strategically placed around the top and bottom of the dress. It was a dress I ordered at last year's Milan Fashion Week and actually never wore. The dress made me feel beautiful, and I needed that right now. I needed to feel empowered as I continued to fight my feelings for Beau. Who knew, maybe I would meet someone else at the party tonight?

I heard the knock on the door so I grabbed my fur coat, leather gloves and clutch bag and opened the door. Beau stood there, looking dapper in his black tuxedo. I took a deep breath as I pretended not to notice just how handsome he looked. Meanwhile, if Beau was trying to hide his reaction to how I looked, he failed miserably. He stood there with a huge smile as his eyes devoured me. "Wow." He said simply.

Set on keeping everything platonic, I put my coat on quickly and locked the door. "Let's go."

In the car, we fell back into an easy and safe conversation. We talked about what we did for Christmas, Beau shared more stories about Oxford and growing up in Buckinghamshire and I shared stories about past New Year's Eve parties. An hour and fifteen minutes later, we were entering the gates of Rose Hall, a seventeenth century three-storey country manor and home to The Warners. "This is gorgeous." Especially done up the way it was tonight. The trees that lined up the long driveway were lit up with fairy lights and the manor looked alive with the party obviously well underway.

"I love my flat in London, but there is nothing like coming home." He smiled as he stopped the car in front of the valet services. He quickly got out and opened the door for me. I took the hand he offered as he helped me out of the car.

He was still holding my gloved hand when we walked into the manor. Beau then made quick work of assisting me out of my coat and gloves, which he then handed over to a servant, and immediately took my hand again as he led me into the crowded ballroom. There, we were immediately met with the lively music played by a twelve-piece band.

I looked around at the elegantly dressed crowd and I felt at home. While there were no seemingly familiar faces, I felt at home in this atmosphere. I had attended many similar parties with my parents. So I wasn't at all nervous until I spied a glum looking older man making his way towards us.

"Good evening, Father." Beau greeted cheerfully when the man stopped in front of us.

"Good to see you, Son." His voice was friendly, however he was frowning as his gaze locked in on Beau holding my hand. I immediately freed my hand and tucked it behind me.

"Father, meet Ruth Triggs. Ruth, this is my father, Israel Warner." We exchanged awkward pleasantries and I was relieved when we were shortly interrupted by a shriek that was audible despite the loud music, "Finally, you're here!"

A beautiful young woman, dressed elegantly in blue, rushed over and Beau hugged her tight. "Yes, kiddo, we're here. Meet my friend, Ruth." He turned to me, "Ruth, this is my little sister, Stephanie."

Stephanie's smile was huge as she looked me over from head to toe. "Call me Steph. You and I are going to get along. I can tell. Come," She linked her arm to mine and pulled me away, then whispered, "Let me save you from Father. I love him but he can be over-protective of his children."

"Beau doesn't need to be protected from me. We're just friends–" I started to explain but was quickly dismissed.

"Sure you are. And that's why my notoriously workaholic brother is all of a sudden bunking off work early? Look, I actually like that Beau is taking time off work. It's good to see he has realised there's more to life than his studies and the hotels."

I was going to insist that Beau and I were just friends, however I remembered that Steph was going to be a lawyer. Deciding that I wasn't up for the debate, I just stayed quiet.

Steph handed me a glass of champagne while she took a glass of soda water for herself. We didn't get too far when we were stopped by Beau's mother. Her silver lacy formal dress made her look unapproachable however her bright grey eyes were friendly and inviting. "I am delighted to finally meet you, Ruth. My son speaks so highly of you."

Taking the opportunity to make it clear that Beau and I were just friends, I answered, "Thank you Mrs. Warner. Beau has been a great friend to me and continues to be a supportive friend."

Mrs. Warner smiled and gave me a look I couldn't quite interpret. "Well I better go and mingle. Enjoy your night, Ruth! And Steph, behave."

I was absolutely enjoying my night. Beau found me shortly after I met his mother and he took me to the corner where his Oxford friends were lounging. Pat was her usual self, the class clown, and she entertained us with hilarious quips and stories. Over canapés and champagne, the jokes got funnier and our laughs got louder.

Half an hour before midnight, the band changed their pace and began to play to slower beat. The mood changed quickly as Colin took Pat's hand and they walked over to the dance floor. Mark and Saskia followed. Left alone, Beau and I sat together in awkward silence for a minute as I kept my eyes on the champagne glass I was holding.

"We should dance." Beau suggested.

"Don't feel like you have to dance with me. This place must be filled with beautiful, single ladies that are waiting for you to invite them to the dance floor." I teased. While my head argued that I couldn't let myself dance with him and get closer to him at the risk of falling deeper in love, my heart skipped a beat at the prospect of a dance.

"Possibly. Yet I find myself wanting to dance with only one lady tonight." Completely charmed and swept off my feet, I took the hand he offered and we walked to the dance floor. Elgar's Salut d'Amour was playing when Beau and I took the dance floor and started a slow waltz.

"You can waltz." Unlike Kane who wouldn't be caught dead doing the waltz.

Beau laughed, "Thank my mother."

Beau drew me closer to him and we continued to dance. At that point, the background faded and it was just Beau and I and the music. It felt amazing to be with him like this. By the time the music ended, I knew I was failing miserably in my pursuit of keeping my feelings for Beau in check.

We were both jolted back to reality when someone bumped into us. I turned to see an intoxicated Chef Leon with his equally intoxicated but stunning wife.

"Ruth! Tu es magnifique." He slurred. "Let's dance." Without waiting for an answer, he took my hand and I had no choice but to dance with him. I could see that Beau was dancing with Chef Leon's wife.

"You're obviously enjoying yourself." I teased playfully.

Chef Leon laughed, "Yes. It is a rare night off so I take advantage! La! The Warners are always gracious hosts, are they not?"

I looked around and indeed, everyone looked like they were having a blast. "It's a great party."

"They are great people. Especially Beau." Then he laughed as he pulled me closer and he whispered in my ear, "Let me tell you a secret, shhh! Ok? I am not supposed to say. The food I give to you from the restaurant, I cook that especially for you because Beau instructed me."

I wasn't sure whether I heard him right. The music was loud and his voice was a whisper. "Beau asked you to provide dinner for us?"

"Oui." He answered. Unclassified emotions whirled within me, but I didn't get the chance to ponder this any further because we were interrupted by the man himself.

"Leon, I am returning your dance partner to you. It's nearly midnight, I am sure you would want her by your side when the clock strikes twelve."

Of course Chef Leon agreed and within a second, I was back in Beau's arms. Before I got the chance to say something, a man took to the microphone on stage and began the countdown from ten and we all joined in.

At exactly midnight, the ballroom windows lit up as fireworks crackled and popped outside. Inside, the band played Auld Lang Syne while everyone was shouting "Happy New Year". Some were raising their glasses, some were kissing their partners and most began waltzing. Beau and I stood there, our eyes glued on each other for minutes. Finally, he bent down his head, nearing his lips to my right ear so that I could hear him, "Happy New Year, Ruth. I know how hard last year was for you. I really wish you the best year ahead. And I'll be here, to make sure it happens." He then turned his head and kissed me on the cheek.

Beau straightened and took me into his arms and led me into the waltz. And as we danced, it dawned on me that he was everything a girl could ask for. He was handsome. He was smart. He was successful. He was thoughtful to the point that he even organised dinner for Mum and I. I still couldn't believe he did that. He was an amazing guy. And he was too good for me. I had nothing to bring to the table. He needed someone that was equally as smart, equally as successful, someone that he would be proud to stand next to. I was nothing, I was no one and I had no future prospects. And because I loved him, I needed to let him find someone that was his equal.

Now, with even more conviction that I needed to distance myself from Beau, I stepped away, "I need to go to the bathroom." And with that excuse, I turned and walked away.

# CHAPTER 14

*I* picked up my clutch bag from the lounge area where we were sitting so I could check my phone on my way to the bathroom. I saw six missed calls from Olivia's friend, Isabelle. Something was wrong. There would be no reason for Isabelle to call me, especially on New Year's Eve. I rushed from the ballroom, in search of a quieter place so I could return the call.

I found myself in the large library. Without noticing more than that, I called Isabelle immediately. She picked up on the second ring, "Ruth! Thank god you've called me back. Olivia was taken to St. Mary's. She must've taken a dirty drug. We just found her on the floor of the Hacienda bathroom."

My heart stopped. Despite all the terrible news that seemed to just keep coming at me these past few months, there really was no preparing for when another came. "Is she... okay?" I couldn't make myself say what I really wanted to know. Had I lost another loved one? No, it could not be so.

"I don't know. They just took her away. I know that you're fighting, but I thought you'd want to know."

"Thank you. I appreciate you calling me. I'll head to the hospital now."

As soon as I hang up, I heard a movement behind me. Steph and a boy were sitting by the fireplace. She quickly stood up and came towards me, "Ruth, what's happened? Are you okay?"

I shook my head, trying not to cry and trying (but failing) not to come to the conclusion that I had also lost Olivia forever. "My sister's been taken to the hospital. I need to go. I need to call a cab."

Steph hugged me, "Oh I am so sorry to hear that. But don't be silly, you're not catching a cab. Let me call Beau. I'm sure he'd want to take you to your sister."

I shook my head, "No, I can't ask him to leave the party -"

Steph interjected with a firm voice, "Ruth, if I let you go in a cab, my brother would kill me. Go get your coat and I'll get Beau to meet you in the foyer." She gave me a quick squeeze then walked away.

I was only too happy to follow instructions at that point. My mind was busy imagining the worse about Olivia's condition. It was a known fact that each time we took pills sourced from dealers we didn't know, we took the risk that it may be dirty. When you're partying though, especially when you're already drunk, you do get careless. I said a silent prayer as I put on my coat and gloves. A second later, I could see Beau running towards me.

Within minutes we were in his car on our way back to London.

Beau seemed to have known that I wasn't up for any conversation, so we stayed quiet throughout the journey. I felt anxious the entire time as I braced myself for the worse. In a way I thought that being prepared for the worse would soften the blow if it did come to that. But of course it also meant that I was starting to live that nightmare in my head and in my heart.

When we neared the hospital, my heart felt like it was pounding outside my chest and my breathing became ragged. Beau took my hand in his. He gave a gentle squeeze and I found myself calming down a little as I looked down at our intertwined hands.

As we approached the main entrance, Beau gave my hand another squeeze, "I'll drop you off at the front and I'll go park the car."

I shook my head, "No. I really appreciate you taking me here, but I can't have you giving up your New Year's for me. Please, Beau, go back to the party. I'm sure-"

"Ruth, allow me to be here for you."

Oh, how I wanted to lean on his strength. But I didn't want to depend on him, to become so reliant on him. We were already too close as it was. No, I needed to create distance between us because nothing has changed since midnight. He deserved better than me. He definitely deserved someone with less drama attached to her. Look at me, I was headed to the hospital yet again. No, it was best that we didn't get too close. "You're an amazing friend, Beau. So much better than I deserve. Please, I insist. Go home. I need to do this alone."

He stopped the car in front of the main entrance. "Please Ruth-"

I released my hand from his, opened the door and with the firmest voice I could muster, I insisted, "Thanks again for taking me here. I can do this on my own." I stepped out and ran to the doors.

Private hospitals were never as manic as public hospitals. In fact they were quite the opposite. As soon as I walked in, I introduced myself and asked after Olivia. I was immediately taken to the relevant ward where the treating doctor met me. Dr. Kerr, a gentle-mannered Irish man, assured me my sister was alive and would pull through. He guided me towards a room where I could see Olivia on the hospital bed through the glass windows. She was asleep.

In his thick accent, Dr. Kerr explained, "We had to sedate her so that we could flush out the toxins. So far, there is no indication that any vital organs have been adversely affected. We will need to monitor her for a few days though, just to be sure." I found myself sighing loudly in relief, however his next words floored me. "Now, as for her baby, it's too early to tell. At the moment the fetus seems to be attached but there is a chance that even if the baby survives, there may still be long term repercussions."

Baby. Fetus. Olivia was pregnant? I was shocked. Out of all the news that might be received, this was one that I had least expected. How far along was she? Did Olivia herself even know she was pregnant? Who was the father? I had so many questions and the only person who could answer them was lying in bed asleep. "I didn't know she was pregnant." I confessed, and even with my own ears, I could hear that my voice was dripped in sadness.

Dr. Kerr patted me on the shoulder like you would a small child. "Now, now, I'm sure she would have eventually told you. It's only early days. Looks about ten weeks, from my calculations."

I nodded as I continued to watch Olivia through the clear windows. Yes, maybe she didn't know. I had to give her the benefit of the doubt that my sister would never knowingly harm her own child. "Can I go to her?" I asked and Dr. Kerr gave his permission.

I walked into the room and headed straight to Olivia who was connected to various machines, her eyes were closed and I could hear her steady breathing along with the steady beeps of machines. Olivia, who was always full of life, looked like life had defeated her. She looked so fragile. So vulnerable. With my ungloved hand, I took her hand as I sat down on the chair next to the bed. I started crying as I continued to look at Olivia, partly from relief – she was going to be okay – and partly from sadness as I acknowledged that our lives were truly separated now.

There was a time that I was the one that Olivia turned to when she had anything going on with her. Big or small. Good or bad.

I continued to hold her hand and I found myself leaning forward and resting my arms and head on the bed as I closed my eyes and said a little prayer. I prayed that Olivia would be okay and that the baby would be too. A sense of peace came over me right before I fell asleep.

I was stirred awake when I felt Olivia snatched her hand from mine. I looked up and found her glaring at me. "What are you doing here?"

I sat up and rotated my aching neck, but I kept my eyes on Olivia and could see that she was seething. I ignored her tone and I smiled at her happily. "I'm so glad you're okay, Olivia."

"I don't want you here. I want you to leave." She folded her arms and turned her face the other way. Sunlight was already filtering through the windows.

"Whatever happens, Olivia, we are still sisters. I love you. I care about you. You nearly died last night. I want to help-"

Olivia laughed bitterly as she turned her vexed eyes on me once again, "How typically predictable you are, Ruth. You are always trying to be the hero, even when we were kids. Oh here comes Ruth to save the day! You just love it when things go wrong because you can swoop in and be everyone's saviour!"

My eyes widened in disbelief. "I did that because I genuinely care!" Yes, it was true that whenever there was anyone in need, I would do anything to ensure I was a shoulder to cry on. I wanted to help them through those tough times. But I didn't do it for me. I couldn't believe Olivia would say such nasty things. "And I care about you, Olivia. A lot. I love you."

"No you don't. You just like being a martyr. But I don't need you."

"Olivia, I know you're pregnant. Let me be there for you."

Her eyes widened and for a second I thought I saw fear in her expression. "I don't need you! Go away!" She was screaming by now and the nurse rushed in to see what was going on. "Nurse, I don't want her here. Take her away."

The nurse looked at me disapprovingly, "Please, Miss, we can't have your sister agitated."

I agreed. I felt defeated. I picked up my gloves, coat and clutch and headed towards the door. Before I exited, I turned back to look at Olivia. And despite everything Olivia had just said, I loved her and I knew I couldn't leave her just yet. I left the room but I parked myself just outside her door, where I could sit and still be able to see inside the room. No, I was sure that once Olivia calmed down, she would remember that we were close once and more than at any time before, she really needed her sister.

Ninety minutes later, I was still sitting outside Olivia's room, nursing a cup of coffee as I continued to watch Olivia who was busy acting like she couldn't see me.

"Ruth!" I turned to see Mum rushing towards me, with Beau trailing just behind her. I stood up and Mum hugged me tight but her eyes were already zeroed in on Olivia through the window. "How's Olivia?"

"She's okay, Mum-" But she wasn't listening as she rushed to Olivia's bedside.

I looked up at Beau, now dressed in casual jeans and a grey sweater. Before he could say anything, I pounced angrily at him, "Why would you tell Mum about Olivia? Mum is recovering so well, this is the last thing she needs right now!"

Beau looked devastated, "I'm sorry, Ruth. I just thought Naomi would want to see Olivia. I didn't think. I should've consulted you first."

Before we could continue, we heard Olivia in hysterics, "Go away! I don't want you here!"

I ran over to Mum as she was saying, "Please, my baby-"

Olivia continued, "You need to accept that we are no longer family! I want you both to leave!"

"Well you heard the young lady." We all turned towards the door where Uncle Mo stood with the doctor and two nurses. "You should leave now and don't come near her again or I'll call the police."

Mum was crying but she didn't move as she looked at Olivia straight in the eye, "I knew what I was giving up when I asked you to stay with your uncle. I accept that I lost the right to be your mother when I entered into that agreement with him. Just know though that I'll never stop loving you." And with a sad smile, she turned around and headed for the door. Uncle Mo stepped aside to let her through.

I gave Olivia a final look of desperation, hoping with all hopes that she would change her mind. But to no avail, Olivia was always a stubborn one. With a sad wave, I followed my mum out of the room.

# CHAPTER 15

"Beau, you should come inside." Mum invited as he stopped his Alfa Romeo in front of our building. I was still annoyed with Beau for telling Mum about Olivia and taking her to the hospital, and now with Olivia's rejection, I was even more worried that it might cause her depression to worsen. She had been doing so well.

I could see that Beau was going to decline the invitation, however Mum continued, "Do you play chess? I would really like to play chess right now but Ruth refuses to play. I guess it brings back memories of her Dad. What do you say, Beau, care to entertain an old woman?"

It wasn't an invitation any caring guy could turn down. So, despite my icy demeanor, Beau walked into the flat with us. Without looking at him, I walked straight to my room. I needed to be by myself. I needed to process everything that had transpired in the past twelve hours.

Still fully clothed in my formal attire from last night, I jumped into bed and closed my eyes. Through the thin walls, I could hear Mum and Beau chatting as they set up the chessboard. I could hear Mum laughing. She didn't seem like she was about to enter the depths of deeper depression. Yet, there I was, continuing to seethe with repressed rage that was squarely focused on Beau.

How could he have been so thoughtless? I was already living in constant fear and apprehension that Mum would relapse. Every single time I walked into the flat after work, a sense of foreboding would grip me only to ease once I saw that my Mum was ok.

About half an hour later it dawned on me that I had used Beau as a proxy for the person I was really angry at. Olivia. I was angry with my sister for rejecting me. I was angry that she was never there when we needed her to be. Then, as I closed my eyes, I remembered how Olivia looked while sedated on that hospital bed. I loved her, despite it all. And so the anger and frustration dissipated gradually.

It was replaced with sadness and concern. Olivia was pregnant. Who was the father? Was he in the picture? Would he support Olivia or was she on her own on this? And even if she was on her own, she didn't want our support. She wanted nothing to do with Mum and I. Yet Olivia was always the more sensible one between us. Yes, we partied but I was always the one that steered her into trouble. I was the wild one.

Then it hit me. I could have been the one in Olivia's situation. In fact, it probably should have been me!

Outside my room, I continued to hear laughter from both Mum and Beau. No longer angry with Beau, I quickly changed into black tights and a loose woolen sweater, pulled my hair into a messy bun and went to join them.

They were sitting at our dining table. I walked over and sat next to Mum. "Beau and I are chasing each other all over the board. It's quite entertaining." Mum had a genuine smile on her face, despite the distressful morning. I watched the interplay between Mum and Beau. He really was a nice guy. He really was perfect.

I could see Beau watching me closely, trying to read my cues. So I looked straight into his eyes and I smiled. I could read relief all over his face and he smiled back and winked.

Within a few seconds he had Mum's king trapped. "Check mate."

Mum clapped her hands. "Great move! Oh we need to play again. I know your moves now."

Beau stood up, "Would love to but I have to go, Naomi, Ruth. My mother is expecting me back home. I'll come back soon for a rematch."

Naomi said her goodbyes, extracting a promise of another game of chess in a couple of days. I walked Beau to the door.

In the hallway, Beau turned around and he gave me a quick hug. "Look, I'm so sorry again that I brought your mum to the hospital. It was thoughtless-"

"Beau, please stop. No need to apologise. You were right to do what you did. It wouldn't have been right for me to keep that a secret from Mum. She had the right to know. Sorry I got so hot-headed."

Beau shrugged, "Understandable. It can't be easy seeing your sister like that. I know you were close to your sister. Are you going to be okay? I could stay if you wanted me to."

I wanted him to stay. But I knew I couldn't let him. Nothing had changed. I didn't deserve him. And I realised, I wanted him to know just how much I didn't deserve him. I wanted him to be the one to walk away because it was getting harder and harder for me to do so. So I confessed, "That should have been me in that hospital bed. I was so much worse that Olivia. If you knew the real me, you wouldn't like me. I'm the wild one. The Party Girl. That's the only thing I was good at. If you really knew the real me, you wouldn't want to be my friend." I walked over to the wall by the door and sat down, dejected. I expected Beau to leave.

He was sensible and responsible, surely the last thing he would want was to be associated with someone like me?

But he didn't leave, instead he knelt down with one leg until our faces were level. He was frowning but his eyes were shining with warmth, "Ruth, don't you realise that's not you anymore? Maybe it never really was. But the moment you decided to stay with your mum… the moment you moved into this place, you stopped being that person. Instead, you're that person that is so loyal that you've stayed with your mum despite how hard life has become. You're that person that is brave enough to walk into The Warner and work until your muscles are sore despite never having worked a day in her life. You're that person that cared enough to make this flat a home. You're that person and so much more. And I'm proud to call you my friend."

I couldn't help it. His words brought tears to my eyes. For the first time, in a long time, I felt like someone was seeing who I really was. "Thank you Beau."

He moved to sit next to me and he put his arm around my shoulders. We sat there, just like that, for what seemed like an eternity. And as we did, I knew that I had fallen even deeper in love with Beau Warner.

A little while later, Beau's phone started ringing. "It's my mother. Did you want me to stay? I'll let her know I'm not coming."

I shook my head. I knew I needed time to talk to Mum about Olivia anyway. "No, you should go. I need some alone time with Mum."

Back in the flat, Mum was sitting on the couch with a cup of tea in her hand. "I really like that boy."

"I like him too, Mum." I sat next to her, tucking my feet under my legs.

"Reminds me of his Dad." Mum said cryptically.

"Mr. Warner? You know Mr. Warner?"

Mum took a sip from her mug and she nodded slowly. "Oh yes, I knew him well. We grew up together and in fact he was my boyfriend for years. We were together for a long time so I guess we just assumed we would eventually get married and start a family. I didn't know I wasn't in love with him until I met your Dad. Once I fell in love I knew that what I felt for Israel was more like brotherly affection than passionate love. Unfortunately, Israel didn't take it well. He wanted nothing to do with me, which is understandable, so we haven't spoken since the day I told him about Eli and I."

"Wait a sec. Before, when you were telling me the story about how you met Dad and you said you were with someone else, that was actually with Beau's father? What a small world." I was floored. Of all people I could have fallen in love with, it happened to be the son of my mum's ex-boyfriend. I suddenly recalled Mr. Warner's cool demeanor last night at the party. "Oh, he must know who I am. It makes sense now why he was a little frosty in his reception last night. I thought it was because he didn't want his son hanging around with their housekeeping staff. Actually, that may also be a reason." I thought.

"I wouldn't think so." Mum answered confidently. "Israel would never be a snob. He doesn't have it in him. I'm willing to bet he knows you're my daughter and you're tainted by association. I wouldn't worry too much, Ruth. It's obvious Beau is in love with you. I wouldn't let that one go, if I were you. Good guys like him are hard to come by."

My heart swelled, "Do you really think he's in love with me? We only ever talk about being good friends."

"Oh he is in love with you. Look how he always makes a point to be around. A guy who just wanted to be just friends wouldn't try so hard."

Excitement rushed through my veins and I found myself unable to breathe as my mind considered the possibility that Beau and I could be together. As I closed my eyes and recalled our tender moments together; that time I poured my grief to him and he listened and he cared enough to want to cheer me up, the laughter we shared while ice skating, the fact that he was always there whenever I needed him, the fun we always had whenever we were together, all those memories welled up and I couldn't deny it any longer. As much I knew I didn't deserve him, I also knew that I wanted him to be mine. And just like that, I gave in to my desires. I knew I was being selfish, but I couldn't help myself. "I'm in love with him too, Mum, but he has never alluded to more than just friendship. But I do want more."

"Then don't let him get away." Mum said matter-of-factly before she took another sip of her tea. Then with a glint in her eye she smiled. "He wants you too but he probably hasn't admitted it to himself or he's too shy to make the first move. Look how beautiful you are, Ruth. You can use that. My advice, kiss him. I'll invite Nora out and you can invite him here, or you can go out for dinner and go someplace afterwards. Just find an opportunity where you can be alone together and kiss him. He won't be able to resist you. Trust me. I know what I'm talking about."

I reddened with embarrassment and nervousness at the thought of being the one to make the first move. I realised that the old Ruth probably wouldn't have hesitated. But the new Ruth, this person who loved Beau and wouldn't want him to be forced into a situation he might not want, this person who cared for Beau and didn't want to ruin their friendship. That person was hesitating. That person was nervous. That person was frightened.

"That's settled then." Mum said. "Now, let's talk about Olivia."

# CHAPTER 16

wo weeks later, I still hadn't gathered up the courage to kiss Beau. However, a plan was forming in my head. The Warners were celebrating Mr. Warner's 50th birthday in town with their family and close friends. The entire staff was abuzz with news of the celebration. Mr. Warner was well loved by his staff so everyone was eager to make this a day he would remember. The plan was to hold an afternoon tea with the hotel employees, followed by pre-dinner drinks with family and friends at The Savoy, the hotel where Mr. Warner's career began, and then dinner in a private restaurant close by so that the party could walk back to The Warner where they were staying the night. Even Beau, who had his own flat in town was to stay at the hotel. My own plans were not so sophisticated – I was to sneak into his room while he was out to dinner and wait for him to get back. While alone, I planned to confess my love and kiss him.

It was the perfect situation and I couldn't let this opportunity pass by.

In the past couple of weeks I'd only seen Beau six times. Four of those times were at work, so there were no real opportunities there! He did come over twice, but both times were to play chess with Mum. Yes, I possibly could have latched onto him every time Mum left the room, but seriously, it wasn't the right atmosphere and every time, I chickened out.

Besides, he continued to act like we were just friends. So here I was, even more confused about how he really felt about me. In the meantime, the past couple of weeks only cemented my feelings for Beau. Every interaction only caused me to fall deeper in love with him despite how innocent and "friendly" those conversations were!

Mum was right. It was time to take our relationship from the friend zone to the romantic zone. And if Beau wasn't the one to take us there, then I would have to be the one to do it. I could do it.

So a few days later, when Mr. Warner's birthday finally came, I woke up a nervous wreck. I literally woke up shaking. I was full of doubts. What if Beau rejected me? What if he laughed at my face? What if he never really liked me in that way? What if it was all an obligation because I was a staff member? What if I was about to make the biggest fool of myself?

I closed my eyes and took a deep breath. I focused my mind on Beau. He was so wonderful. He was worth taking the risk. Flirtations and seduction used to be so easy for me, it was second nature. I knew I was pretty and I knew I attracted male attention so easily. I needed to tap into that old part of me. Surely Beau wouldn't be able to resist?

"Ruth, are you awake?" Mum walked in with a tray of toast and orange juice. Mum had been bringing me breakfast in bed quite often lately. I knew it was her way of saying 'sorry' for what she put me through a few months ago.

"Thanks Mum, you know you don't need to keep bringing me breakfast in bed, right?" I sat up and helped Mum balance the tray on my lap.

Mum nodded, "I know. But I enjoy doing it."

I smiled and I nervously confessed my plans to Mum, "Today's the day, Mum. I'm going to tell Beau how I feel."

"About time! Good luck, but I know you won't need it. Beau loves you, he's just too scared to admit it" She winked and then walked out.

Clinging to Mum's assurances that Beau loved me. I quickly devoured my breakfast and got ready for work.

The morning was just like any other morning. I went through my cleaning routine just like any other day. But at lunch, instead of eating at the common room, I headed to the shops. Even though I knew I couldn't really afford it, I needed something that would give me courage – a new sexy outfit! Besides, what sane guy could ever resist a woman in tight clothing? Especially the red dress I ended up purchasing. Courage and excitement was growing within me. I knew I looked smoking hot in that red dress.

The afternoon tea held with The Warner staff kicked off at 3pm in the hotel lobby, which was decorated with balloons and confetti. Delicate sandwiches, pastries, coffee and tea were served generously as we all gathered around Mr. Warner and his family. I stood towards the back of the crowd as Chef Leon and his team wheeled in a huge four-tiered cake and we all began to sing 'Happy Birthday'. This was then followed by Mr. Warner's speech in which we thanked everyone and expressed how he thought of all of us as family. Throughout this, Beau stood by his father with a big smile on his face. My heart contracted at the thought that by the end of the day, if it all went according to plan, Beau and I would be together.

Once the formalities ended, Nora walked over to me with a fresh cup of tea, "What are you doing this afternoon? A few of us are thinking of continuing the celebration at the pub. You should come!" I nodded quickly and accepted the invitation. I wasn't sure what I was going to do with myself between now and later tonight so this invitation was perfect.

"Ruth! So good to see you again! How's your sister?" Steph came over and she gave me a quick hug.

"Hi Steph! Olivia's fine. To be honest, she's not really talking to me right now despite all my efforts, so I don't know for sure, but I do know she's out of the hospital and she's staying at our Uncle's estate in Worcester."

"Well I'm glad to hear she's fine, at least." Steph said sympathetically.

"Who's fine?" This time, it was Beau who joined us. He stood just behind me and so I had to step back to make room for him in the circle. I looked up and our eyes met. He smiled a greeting and childishly pulled my ponytail softly. "Are you fine?"

"Yes, I'm fine. Are you fine?" I countered as we continued to smile at each other.

Steph cleared her throat, "Glad to hear you're both fine. Nora and I are fine too, thanks for asking." She said sheepishly, then her eyes widened, "Oh and you know who else is fine? Father and Mother, and here they come now."

Sure enough, Mr. and Mrs. Warner stopped by and Nora and I echoed our "Happy Birthday".

"Thank you." Mr. Warner replied. "Nora, how's the family?"

"They are good, Sir. Their school report cards have improved so I am very happy." Nora replied and Mr. Warner laughed.

"That is good to hear! Now, Beau and Steph, come join us, let's mingle." Mr. Warner's tone didn't leave room for arguments, and besides, it was his birthday.

Beau winked at me and he turned to follow his family to the next group.

I was decidedly dismissed by Mr. Warner. Was it because of his history with my mum or was it because Beau and I had gotten too close for his liking? Shrugging it off, I took a deep breath to steady myself. I couldn't let this stop me from tonight's mission.

"Well that was awkward." Nora said, stating the obvious.

"Sure was." I shrugged, trying to act like I didn't care.

"I think I know why." She said with a secret smile. I didn't get a chance to pry the answer from Nora as we were interrupted by Joy who was serving slices of the birthday cake.

I said my goodbyes a few minutes after 8pm. For those that joined the unofficial after-party, the fun and merriment was still in full flight. However, for me, three cocktails later, it was finally time to act. I walked back to The Warner, taking extra care not to be spotted by other staff members. I grabbed my secret weapon (the red dress) from my locker, the masterkey from the office and walked towards the service lift. I already knew which room Beau was allocated. There were five premier one-bedroom suites and he was allocated the park-facing suite on the top floor.

My heart was racing. I was nervous. Of course I had a ready excuse just in case someone asked me what I was doing. No one would say anything if I say I had left something behind. But still, I was a ball of hot nerves at the prospect of being caught out.

I was so relieved when I didn't encounter a soul throughout the short journey to Beau's room. When I got close to the door, I ran towards it, used the master-key card to unlock it and hurriedly let myself in.

The suite consisted of a lounge with a dining area and a bedroom with an ensuite. I spotted Beau's overnight bag on the sofa and the clothes he was wearing this afternoon was piled neatly beside his bag. He had obviously already used the room to get ready for dinner. An open bottle of red wine and a used wine glass sat on the coffee table. The bottle was still practically full so Beau must have had only half a glass before he left for dinner. I walked around the suite slowly. I picked up the shirt Beau had worn, it still smelt like him. My heart skipped a beat as I dreamt of Beau's arms around me.

I looked at the time. 8:45pm. Mr. Warner's dinner started at 7pm so I would expect Beau back in his room around 10pm. This was perfect. It gave me time to get ready.

I headed for the bedroom and the ensuite and I took a shower to freshen up. After three cocktails at the pub, I was feeling a little worse for wear. Obviously my body wasn't so used to alcohol nowadays!

After a long shower, I took the time to dry my hair until it sat perfectly on my shoulders. After, I used the hotel moisturizer on my skin, donned my new dress and applied make up on my face. As minutes ticked by, the gravity of what I was about to do suddenly hit me hard. I was so in love with Beau. I had never felt like this before. Not even with Kane. And I realised that I would be beyond devastated if Beau rejected me. My nervousness resurfaced ten-folds and I found myself sitting down on the edge of the bath unable to breathe. I was having a panic attack!

It took an entire ten minutes for me to calm myself down. But the nervous tension in the pit of my stomach stayed. Slowly standing up, I knew what I needed, more fuel to give me courage because a huge part of me was ready to run away. I was regretting this idiotic plan. Why couldn't I have just tried to kiss him when I walked him to the door when he came to visit? That would have been simpler! Why did I have to make such a grandiose plan that could easily backfire?

I walked over to the empty wine glass and red wine bottle that Beau had abandoned and I poured myself a glass. I sat on the sofa sipping wine, trying to think positive. Mum was so sure Beau was in love with me. I catalogued our past interactions in my head; I had to admit that there was a part of me that thought that too or I wouldn't be here. I found myself pouring another glass of wine as courage built up within me.

Half an hour later, I went to pour myself another glass only to realise the bottle was empty. Oh boy, I had polished off a whole bottle of wine by myself. And suddenly I didn't feel too well. I looked at the time. Nearly 10pm. Beau should be here soon. I needed to check myself in the mirror, one last time. I stood up and found myself stumbling toward the bedroom. The room was spinning around me. I only made it to the bed. I needed to sit down.

As I sat on his bed, the room continued to whirl and my stomach churned and combined with my ongoing nervousness, I suddenly felt ill. I slowly lay down and closed my eyes. I just needed to rest a second and I was sure I'd feel better.

"Ruth? Ruth, are you okay?" A voice reverberated within my consciousness. It was Beau's voice. Beau! The very man I was waiting for! I opened my eyes and saw Beau bending over me, worry etched in his eyes.

"Beau!" I quickly sat up and winced when I realised I still felt ill. But the show must go on. I didn't get this far only to back out now. I trained my eyes back onto Beau and caught him as his gaze zeroed in on my attire. Emboldened, I stumbled out of bed and wrapped my arms around his neck. "Beau, I've been w-waiting for youuuu." Even with my own ears, I could hear that I was slurring, but I kept going, "I've fallen in love with you." I went on my tiptoes and moved to kiss him. But Beau stepped back, forcing me to break my embrace. He held my forearms as he kept me at a safe distance.

"Ruth, you're drunk. I'm not taking advantage of you in this state."

"But I love you." I declared, and as it dawned on me that Beau was rejecting me, my voice took on a tinge of desperation. "Don't you love me? I thought if I kissed you, you'd realise that you were in love with me, or at least if you didn't already love me that you would fall in love with me…" I stepped away from him and sat down on the bed. I was starting to feel like I needed to throw up. I wasn't sure whether it was from the alcohol or the rejection. I felt horrible. I truly felt sick.

Beau knelt down in front of me and held my hand. "Don't you realise that you are worth so much more than this? Yes, you're beautiful and you're incredibly sexy, but you are so much more than that. You are clever, loyal, funny, strong, patient and so much more than I can ever put into words. You don't need to go through these extremes to make me fall in love with you because-"

At this point I had already stopped listening as my body gave in. I was really going to be sick. I reached for the bin under the bedside table and I threw up. Beau held my hair away from my face as I continued to vomit for what seemed like forever.

That exercise thoroughly depleted what little energy I had left. Immediately, my eyes grew heavy and all I could think about was sleep. I felt Beau tuck me into bed and the last thought in my head as I drifted off to sleep was that Beau and I were in the middle of a conversation. We needed to finish the conversation. I couldn't quite remember what it was about. But I knew it was important. Tomorrow. We'd finish talking tomorrow.

# CHAPTER 17

*I* was wide awake in an instant and it didn't take long at all for my brain to recall exactly where I was and what had happened the night before. Beau had rejected me. He didn't love me, after all. As my mind replayed the entire episode, my whole body, from the roots of my hair to the tips of my toes, turned red - matching the dress perfectly - with pure shame and humiliation, and as memories of last night continued to wash over me, wave after wave, I found myself cringing with absolute horror. Oh my god, the benefit of hindsight, this really was such a bad idea. Beau never wanted me. It was just friendship on his part. Now, not only had I humiliated myself, I was also hurting with his rejection. My heart, which had already taken a beating in the past months, was shattered yet again. It was all too much. I wanted to bury myself and forget this whole thing ever happened.

The clock by the bedside table signaled 7am. I needed to get out of here. Now. Pronto. I slowly raised my head to check if Beau was around. He wasn't in the bedroom. Relieved, I got up oh so quietly, not wanting to make any noise just in case Beau was in the next room. I found my stuff in the ensuite, I covered my dress with my parka, put my boots on, gathered my things and crept out of the bedroom.

I could see Beau asleep on the sofa. He had taken a spare pillow and blanket and there he was, fast asleep. Oh, what must he think of me? Surely he wouldn't want anything to do with me now, not even as friends. I really needed to get out if there before he woke up. I continued to tip-toe towards the exit and as quietly as I could, I opened the door and got out of there.

I couldn't wait to get home and pretend this whole nightmare never happened. Yet I knew that this was a memory I would never forget. The man I loved rejected me. It was the first time I had been rejected like that. Normally guys would jump at the chance to kiss me. But not Beau. I guess I wasn't pretty enough to tempt him. Why did I think he would have wanted me anyway? Of course he himself knew he was too good for the likes of me. What made it worse was that I proved to him just how worthless and embarrassing I was by allowing myself to get drunk and then vomit in front of him. Yes, my pride had taken a beating, but it was my heart I was worried about. Beau's rejection hurt. It really did. I could feel tears running down my eyes as I took a seat in the tube. And it hurt more to think that he wouldn't want anything to do with me now. I had ruined everything.

About half an hour later, I entered our building and headed up the stairs. When I got to my floor, I was surprised to see Kane walking towards me. He had his usual swagger and he looked as cute as ever. "Ruth! There you are! I was hoping to see you before you left for your shift but it looks like you were on the night shift…?" Kane walked over and he kissed my cheek as a greeting.

I was confused. My mouth was literally hanging open because the last time I saw Kane he didn't want anything to do with me. "What are you doing here, Kane?" My tone carried stress and frustration. Kane was the last person I expected to see and this was the last thing I needed right now. I just wanted to crawl into bed and die.

"Babe, I'm here because I love you and miss you." He stepped closer. "I was an idiot, I shouldn't have let you go. I am so sorry, Ruth, please forgive me. I want you back."

I just stood there with my mouth still wide open. His words shocked me. They actually left me speechless.

Not deterred by my silence, Kane continued, "I'd do anything to have you back, Ruth. I'm serious. I've even spoken to my dad about this. He's agreed to get us a house in Cambridge so your mum can come live with us. He's also agreed to pay for your tuition if you still wanted to go to university. If not, that's okay too, I can look after you and your mum. You can just stay home and be with your mum. Please Babe, let me take care of you. Let me take you away from this place."

I hadn't even began to process what Kane had just said when I found myself being taken into his arms. I found myself even more stunned than ever before. Kane just offered me the world. I knew it was an offer too good to pass up. But I also knew one important thing. I didn't love him. In fact, I never loved him. I now knew what real love was but unfortunately the man I loved didn't love me back. Oh a small part of me rejoiced at the thought that at least someone wanted me. And that was probably why I allowed Kane to hug me longer than I knew was right.

"Kane, I can't." I really couldn't. Even though Beau didn't want me, I was still in love with him. I would continue to still love him. That much I was certain. So it wasn't fair on Kane. "Your offer is beyond generous. But I'm not in love with you-"

"Are you with someone else?" Kane asked, crossing his arms defensively.

I shook my head, "No, I'm not. But it doesn't mean I'm available, Kane. I'm not in love with you. It wouldn't be fair on you."

Kane shook his head and he took my hand. "I take the blame for that, Babe. I rejected you, abandoned you. I know I hurt you. But I was so wrong to do that. I was able to make you fall in love with me before, I am confident I can do it again. Give us a chance, Ruth. You won't regret it. I can take you away from here." And suddenly, Kane knelt down on one knee, he took a small purple velvet jewelry box from his jacket pocket and revealed a huge diamond ring. It was an impressive ring. "I love you Ruth. Let me spend the rest of my life proving to you just how much. Marry me." Unexpectedly, he pulled me to him until I sat on his knee then his kissed me.

I didn't move. Instead my mind processed my response. Having just experienced rejection myself, I knew how much it hurt and I wouldn't wish it on anyone let alone someone I cared about deeply at one point in my life. But it needed to be done. So after a second, I pulled away and I chose my words carefully to soften the blow, "Kane, you do me such great honour, but I can't marry you-"

I stopped when the door to my flat flew wide open. Mum stood there with tears in her eyes, "Ruth, please say 'Yes'! You deserve to be happy. He can take you away from this dreadful place. You don't have to work in that hotel anymore. You can go back to studying. I'll come with you. Kane can look after us. "

Kane straightened up, "Listen to your mum, Ruth. I'm not saying we should marry straight away. I know we're far too young. I just wanted to show you how serious I am about this. Really, my wish is for us to pick up where we left off. You can be that care-free girl again, we can party, have fun together and when the time is right we'll get married."

There was a time that this would have been everything I could have hoped for. Kane was offering me a chance to live my old life but also be able to care for Mum at the same time. The best of both worlds.

Yet I wasn't even tempted. Not even a little. I knew then that I genuinely didn't want my old life back. Before, I stayed because of Mum - because she needed me. But now I was staying because I knew this was exactly where I was supposed to be. I didn't want my old life back. Of course, I would love to have Dad, Kyle and Mark back. But I didn't want that life where I lived for nothing of substance. There was more to life than that. I didn't know exactly what my next step was; I just knew there was no going back. As much as I was hurting right now because of Beau's rejection, I was even more convinced that Kane was not the answer. He wasn't my future.

"We can't pick up where we left off because I'm a different person now. I've changed. Kane, I can't go with you. Mum and I are staying. I'm sorry, but this is really goodbye." And to emphasise my point, I turned and walked away. I walked into the flat, closed the door and I didn't look back.

Mum stood by the closed door, her eyes wide with disbelief. "What have you done? Kane was so generous! I'm sure it didn't go well with Beau because when Kane asked you if you had someone else you didn't mention him so why would you turn down a chance for us to escape-"

"Mum, we're going to be okay. I know we are. Yes, Beau didn't want me…" as I said those words out loud for the first time, I found myself crying. Oh how the truth hurt! I could feel the pain etched deep within my soul. "Beau wasn't in love me, after all. But Mum, we are going to get through this together. I don't love Kane. It's not right for me to use him just because of what he can offer us." I hugged Mum, "It's going to be okay." Even as I said those words, my heart rejected it. Oh I knew I made the right decision regarding Kane but my heart was still sick from Beau's rejection and the humiliation from the entire episode. To make it worse,

I couldn't turn to the one person who was always there for me, the one person who cheered me up.

"We're going to be okay." I repeated. I knew Mum and I were going to be okay. But I didn't know if I could say the same thing about my heart.

# CHAPTER 18

*I* spent the rest of the day in bed, binge watching on Netflix, grateful that I had a couple of days off work so I could just retreat from reality even just for a little bit. Not that it worked perfectly because any hint of sadness in those episodes triggered an over-inflated bout of tears.

Yet there was a part of me that remained hopeful – of what, I wasn't quite sure. Maybe I was hopeful that last night was a big misunderstanding and Beau was in love with me after all, or that he would come around and think the whole thing was funny and we would go on as friends. Whatever it was, there was a part of me that kept my phone charged and close by. Just in case.

But there were no messages or calls from Beau that day. Or the next day. However Mum was determined to get me out of bed and she even went as far as to use her illness to trigger me into action. She apparently needed me to go with her to her appointment with Dr. Campbell. So I went with her early that morning and as we walked into Dr. Campbell's practice, we found the reception desk empty despite the phone ringing incessantly. Did Kat step out for a few minutes? Dr. Campbell's office door was closed, signaling that she was in session.

We were fifteen minutes early for Mum's appointment so we sat down by the fire, and waited.

The phone at reception started ringing again. It rang out. A few minutes later it rang and rang out yet again. Where was Kat? When the phone rang a third time, I found myself jumping up and instinctively picking up the phone. "Dr. Campbell's office, how can I help you?"

"Oh hi, Kat. How are you today?" A man's voice greeted kindly.

"I'm sorry, this is Ruth on the phone. Kat doesn't seem to be in at the moment, so I am just filling in."

"Oh right. Well hi Ruth. I have an appointment with Dr. Campbell today but I will need it rescheduled for next week."

Knowing I wouldn't be able to access Kat's computer to check the schedule, I simply answered, "Alright, let me jot down your request. I don't have access to the schedule right now so we'll return the call to confirm the appointment next week. Can I get your name and phone number?" I wrote down the details on the pad sitting on Kat's reception desk.

As soon as that call ended, the phone rang yet again. This time, a woman complained that she had been trying to call since yesterday as she needed an appointment with Dr. Campbell so she could get her medication refilled. I soothed the patient easily. After working in housekeeping, you learnt how to deal with complaints quite easily. I added her details onto the pad paper and promised to call her back.

"That was amazing! You handled that so well!" Dr. Campbell stood behind me just outside her office door, clapping her hands in applause.

"Dr. Campbell!" Even while Dr. Campbell was obviously complimenting me, I felt guilty about answering the calls. It wasn't something a patient's family member should be doing while waiting at reception.

Dr. Campbell quickly said her goodbye to the patient she had just finished with and greeted Mum who was by now standing close by. Dr. Campbell then turned back to me with a big smile. "Ruth, Mrs. Hopkins is quite a difficult character. I don't need to listen to the whole conversation to be able to tell that you were able to smooth her ruffled feathers, so thank you! And thank you for stepping in."

"Not a problem. I'm happy to help. Is Kat sick?" I inquired.

Dr. Campbell sighed as she responded, "No, Kat's boyfriend is heading back home to Australia and she's going with him. I'm happy for her but it meant that she needed to pack up and go rather quickly so there was no time for me to look for a replacement -" Then suddenly, Dr. Campbell's face lit up. "But I'm certain that I'm looking at her replacement right now."

"Me?" I couldn't believe it. Was Dr. Campbell really offering me a job as her receptionist? "But I don't know anything about being a receptionist." I admitted. Then realised that I should have acted more confidently. This actually sounded like a great opportunity!

Mum stepped in. "Ruth, you'll be amazing at it. You're amazing with people and you're sensitive to their needs. You should consider it."

"Yes, Ruth. Please do consider it. I have a feeling it will come naturally to you. I'll take your mum in now and while we're in there, just think about it. And if you need longer to consider the offer, that's fine too. But let me tell you this now, I promise I will pay you well and I'm sure the hours will be shorter than what you're doing now at The Warner." With a big smile, she turned and ushered Mum into her office.

It was a tempting job offer. But taking the job also meant that I would probably never see Beau again. Maybe that was a good thing? Yet my heart ached at that thought. No, even if he didn't love me, staying at The Warner would at least mean that we could possibly rebuild our friendship at some point in the future. Besides, I couldn't let Nora down. She couldn't have another resignation.

The phone rang again. This time, it was a patient just wanting to say hello. This man was lonely and this one phone call was possibly his only human connection that day. So we chatted about the weather, what the prime minister was up to these days and how amazing Australia would be for Kat. By the time that phone call ended, I knew I was going to take the job. This was a place where I could make a real difference to the lives of the patients. I had always been great at connecting with people and now I knew that I could channel that to help those in real need.

It also hit me that I needed to take control of my future. I couldn't just stay at The Warner simply because I was in love with the owner. I couldn't and wouldn't put my life on hold in hopes that one day he would love me too. I needed to grab hold of this amazing opportunity that had fallen on my lap. And I also knew deep down, Nora would be happy for me. She would encourage me to take the job.

As soon as Dr. Campbell opened the door to her office, I jumped up and hopped over to give my answer, "I'll take the job. Thank you so much for giving me this opportunity, Dr. Campbell!"

There was a rush of celebrations all round. Mum gave me a huge hug, Dr. Campbell literally danced for joy and I laughed at how happy the news made them. Inside, I was excited at this new bend in the road yet there was a sense of sadness as I acknowledged that this really was also a goodbye to The Warner. The work may have been hard, but the people were amazing. I was going to miss them all. Except for Nora, she was our neighbor so we were sure to stay friends.

"So, when can you start? As you can see, I need you sooner rather than later." Dr. Campbell urged.

"In a fortnight." I answered. I needed to give Nora a week's notice.

"Brilliant. Come, if you have a little bit of time now, we can go over the job a little bit more?"

So both Mum and I sat down with Dr. Campbell as we discussed what the job entailed and agreed on a salary that was significantly higher than what I was currently earning.

As Mum and I walked out into the streets, Mum squeezed my hand and smiled. "You did the right thing yesterday. I urged you to go with Kane out of fear. I was afraid that I had ruined your future and there was a chance to get you back on track. But I was wrong. I see now that you are right. We are both on this path for a reason. And today, I am witness to you coming into your own. I have a feeling that this path is going to lead you to your destiny. I am so excited for you! I'm proud of you."

I couldn't help but get teary in response. Funnily enough, I felt the same way. It was a feeling that I was stepping into my future. I didn't know what that looked like yet, but I had a feeling that I just made a significant step towards it.

# Chapter 19

The very next day, I walked into The Warner a little earlier than usual. It was bound to be a big day for me. Today was the day I was going to hand-in my resignation. Nora would already be in so I headed straight to her office and after a gentle knock at her door, I heard Nora say, "Come in!"

I opened the door and saw Nora digging through her large black Michael Korrs bag. "Oh Ruth, it's you! Come in, come in. Don't mind me, I'm just looking for my chapstick, my lips are dry – aha! There it is!" Setting her bag down, she turned to me, "Okay, so what's up?"

By now I was seated at her desk. I was nervous. I loved Nora as I do a close friend. She had been so good to me and I felt as though I was letting her down. She was always complaining about being down staff numbers. Suddenly, my lips also felt dry, so I licked them before I began. "Nora, I have news. Yesterday, I took Mum to Dr. Campbell's office and Kat, the receptionist-"

"I remember her! Yes, the cute one with the Aussie boyfriend." Nora added.

"Yes, that's the one. Well she's decided to follow her boyfriend to Australia so the receptionist role became available and Dr. Campbell offered it to me."

Before I could continue, Nora stood up, placed her hand on her hips and interrupted me once again, "Ruth Triggs, please tell me you accepted that job!"

"Yes I did. I swear, I didn't apply for the job, it was just given to me-" I explained but this was drowned by a very loud (and long!) squeal of delight from Nora as she rushed towards me.

Nora was just about to give me a hug when her office door opened. "What's all this noise about?" We looked up to see Beau at the door. I also saw the moment he saw me in the room because his face turned from inquisitive to... horror? Maybe even dismay?

Nora started dancing around, her arms swinging up and down in the air, "Congratulations are in order for our dear Ruth! She is moving on to bigger and better things!"

Beau merely nodded. Then with a small and an obviously forced smile, he uttered a quick, "Congratulations, Ruth. I wish you well." Then he turned around and left.

Nora stopped dancing as a frown settled on her brows. "Someone is obviously going to miss you. Don't mind him. Men react so weird sometimes."

What Nora didn't know was the truth behind why Beau reacted the way he did. He couldn't even look at me. He was obviously horrified and embarrassed about how I acted the other night and he wanted to make it absolutely clear to me that he didn't return my feelings. As if his rejection that night wasn't clear enough! Whatever hope I was holding onto shattered at that moment. Tears started to form around my eyes and I couldn't hold them back.

"My dear, why are you crying? If it's because of Beau, I'm sure he'll come 'round." I couldn't say a word, I was ashamed of how I behaved so there was no way I was going to tell Nora what was really going on. So I just sat there and continued to cry. Given Nora's small stature, she didn't need to bend down to give me a hug and we stayed like that for a few minutes while I cried it out.

"Okay, my dear, let's be happy now. You have happy news, and I for one, am so proud of you. I'm happy that I could be there to help you when you needed help but I always knew your time here was temporary. And now, you have a better job offer, well that is great news so we should be happy and celebrate! I will organise drinks for you after work so we can par-taay!" I forced a smile on my face and nodded. It was always going to be difficult coming face to face with Beau for the first time after that "incident". I was glad, at least, it was over and done with now. Besides, Nora was right. I should be happy. This was the beginning of a new chapter in my life. However impossible it was going to be, I needed to pull myself together and just get on with it. Taking a deep breath, I agreed to drinks after work.

We talked a little bit more about the new job until it was time for me to start my shift. As I walked out of Nora's office, I was apprehensive just in case Beau was around. The last thing I wanted was another awkward encounter with Beau. His door remained firmly closed. Breathing a sigh of relief, I rushed out of the office area and headed towards the staff lockers.

Less than half an hour later, I was changing bed sheets when I saw Beau walk in. He was the last person I expected to see. I dropped the bed sheets and just stared at him.

"Ruth, I wanted to apologise for the way I acted this morning. It was childish and disingenuous and you deserve better than that."

I couldn't believe he was apologising to me. "I'm the one that should be apologising, Beau. I'm so sorry about the other night-"

He held up his hand to stop me, "Please don't apologise. We don't have to talk about it. I just wanted to congratulate you and say goodbye."

I stared at him for a few seconds. I'd never seen this side of Beau. I could tell he was wearing a mask and he wasn't allowing me to see beyond the surface. "We don't have to say goodbye. I won't be too far away."

"But I will be. We have a new hotel opening in Athens and I'm heading there indefinitely so I can oversee the renovation and then manage it."

"You're going to live in Greece? When do you leave?" I asked. The news was like a kick in the gut. Yes, I already knew there was no future for Beau and I, yet I really had hoped…

"Today. Now. There's been delays over there so I need to sort it out quickly."

I wanted to cry. It was all so sudden. "What about your studies?" It was the first thought as my head tried to find reasons for Beau to stay.

He shrugged casually, "I'm in my last semester now, so I'll study by correspondence and come back for my final exams." His voice was so neutral, so matter of fact, which for me highlighted further that he never really cared about me in that way. I walked away from the bed and closer to Beau so I could see his face - his eyes - clearly. I couldn't read the emotions that lurked behind his eyes. All I knew was that it wasn't sadness. If he had even an ounce of feelings for me, surely he would be sad to be saying 'goodbye'? How did I ever think that there was a chance he loved me? He was a kind and generous man and I misinterpreted his kindness and generosity for love. I was such a fool. I was the reason he was leaving. I must have really embarrassed him and myself with my confession of love, albeit a drunken one! Was it really that bad that he had to leave town?!

My pride kicked into gear. Wanting to mirror his nonchalant demeanor, I merely nodded and replied, "Well I guess this is goodbye."

"I guess it is." Beau agreed before saying, "Goodbye Ruth. I really do wish you well." His eyes stayed on my face for a few seconds before he turned around for the door.

As he was turning away, I swear I spied sadness wash over his expression. "Beau-" I found I couldn't just let him just walk away.

But when he turned back around, his mask was back on. "Yes?"

In an act of utter desperation that I could not control, I found myself saying, "I thought we're friends. Don't friends hug each other when they're saying their farewell?" I sounded desperate and I found myself cringing with embarrassment. And as moments passed and Beau didn't move a muscle, I realised that I placed myself yet again in a situation of rejection. As if that first rejection wasn't bad enough! I was obviously a glutton for punishment.

Suddenly, Beau walked towards me and within seconds I was in his arms. It was awkward at first, his arms were stiff around me, but as I hugged him back, he started to loosen up. I had to admit, it still felt good to be in Beau's arms. Shamelessly, I hugged him tighter, cherishing what I knew was going to be the last time I would feel his arms around me.

"Goodbye, Ruth." Beau whispered into my ear and then he kissed the area above my ear. He pulled away and as he did I could see pain reflected in his eyes.

I wanted to ask him to stay. I wanted to ask him to stick around because maybe he would learn to love me. But I didn't. Because I didn't have the boldness nor the fortitude to be hurt more than I was already hurting. "Goodbye, Beau." I whispered back, but he was already gone. I sat down on the bed and cried my eyes out.

# CHAPTER 20

"We will see you in a fortnight, Mrs. Bennett." I smiled warmly at the immaculately dressed woman in her fifties who had just finished a session with Dr. Campbell. The woman waved goodbye before making her exit.

"Well, that's the last session of the day. Let's do our filing, pack up and we can both head home." Dr. Campbell walked back to her office to tidy up. It was my fifth day on the new job so I knew the drill. I opened up the online file saved on our shared drive from Mrs. Bennett's session, I noted a couple of items I needed to action from Dr. Campbell's notes, efficiently got onto them and I filed the notes where they belonged. Within half an hour, I had also tidied up the office and we were ready for Monday.

"I'm all set!" I declared as Dr. Campbell walked out of her office with her handbag.

"That's awesome. You are doing an amazing job, Ruth. Great first week on the job, it's like you've been here forever. You are a natural, especially when it comes to dealing with our patients." Dr. Campbell came over and gave me a warm hug. "I am so happy you took the job. Thank you."

"I'm so grateful you gave me the opportunity, Dr. Campbell. Thank you again." I replied with a huge smile. This relationship was fast becoming a genuine mutual admiration society. Dr. Campbell took every opportunity to express her gratitude and her high regard for me and I did the same.

We locked up and Dr. Campbell got in the lift to pick up her car in the basement car park and I walked down the stairs to walk to tube. I hadn't taken more than a couple of steps out of the building when I heard my name being called out. I looked up to see Eve, my former best friend, making her way towards me in the crowd.

Eve looked as gorgeous as ever; her platinum blonde hair was curled perfectly and you couldn't fault her outfit. "I knew that was you! Oh my god, Ruth! How the hell have you been?" Eve exclaimed loudly, making a big display as she gave me a big hug and kissed me on both cheeks. "It has been a millennium since I last saw you."

Surprisingly, I didn't feel any bitterness or animosity towards Eve. Yes, she abandoned me at a time I needed someone most desperately, but I now knew just how shallow and fake that life really was. Her abandonment was freedom. So instead of a cutting remark, I merely said, "Yes, It has been a long time."

I could see Eve's eyes scanning me from head to toe. But again, I didn't care. I was happy with the way I looked; my hair was pulled up in a neat ponytail, I wore a navy blue suit and a simple white blouse – it may not be Armani, but I liked how I looked. She blinked and any judgment or cattiness disappeared as her face again took on a friendly demeanor. "So how are you?" She asked as we both stepped to the side of the building so we could chat properly.

"I'm doing well, Eve. I work here now," I pointed to the building. "I'm a receptionist-slash-assistant for a psychologist. I love it."

"Wow, that's amazing." Eve quickly brushed over my answer, obviously keen to get onto the real topic she wanted to talk about. "So I hear you're fighting with your sister?"

"I guess you can say that." I shrugged, not really wanting to engage in this conversation. I still worried about Olivia, but all my messages to her remained unanswered. I even tried to visit her a couple of times at the townhouse, only to be sent away.

"Well I would be furious with her too, if I were you! It's the ultimate betrayal! I know that you and Kane were broken up, but still, to get herself pregnant with his baby is just low. How desperate can you get?"

My heart stopped. I couldn't breathe as my mind, body and soul tried to process what Eve was saying. Surely not? Surely Kane was not the father of Olivia's baby? Eve must be lying.

"Oh my god, don't tell me you didn't know?" Eve gasped, her hand on her lips. I didn't answer. "But everyone knows! Our whole circle knows."

"I'm out of the circle so I guess no one thought to tell me." I whispered, leaning onto the building wall for support. My knees suddenly felt weak. I was hurt, how could Olivia shack up with Kane? She couldn't have known that I was no longer in love with Kane so she had done that with the knowledge that I could very well have been still in love with him.

"Well I guess now you know." Eve shrugged. "So what are you going to do?" She asked, looking very much like she was enjoying the drama that was unfolding before her.

Not wanting to feed more fuel into the gossip mill, I took a few seconds to try to collect myself. Then, when I felt a little more in control, I shrugged, faking nonchalance, "She's welcome to him. I realised I was never really in love with Kane."

Eve frowned, obviously disappointed with my reaction. "Really, Ruth? No grand plans for vengeance? You're not mad?"

"No, not at all. Shocked, yes. But not mad."

Eve harrumphed in disgust and she turned away, "Look, I better go. It was nice to bump into you though."

Once Eve was gone, I walked back into the building and sat myself down on the set of sofas just by the entranceway. There, my emotions let loose. Of course I was mad. I felt betrayed by my own sister. How dare her be mad at me when I was the one with the right to be angry! How dare her push me away when I should be the one pushing her away? I grabbed my phone from my bag and angrily typed Olivia a message, "Is it true? Kane is the father?"

I watched as the message turned from 'Delivered' to 'Read'. My blood boiled as I could see her typing then stopping then typing again. Finally I got a message back, "Yes."

That was it? Just 'Yes'? No 'I'm sorry', no explanations? I felt my anger move to another level. But then I got another message from Olivia, "But he doesn't want me. He wants you." With that message my anger dissipated and I acknowledged something that I had always known but had refused to consider. Olivia had been in love with Kane from the very beginning. The looks she threw Kane's way should have given me a clue. Unrequited love. Rejection. Those were all too familiar to me. I knew just how much that hurt. I knew just how much it consumed you. Poor Olivia!

I typed a message back. "I know what it's like to love someone who doesn't love you back. I'm sorry."

"You're not angry? You don't hate me?" Olivia messaged.

"No." I couldn't hate my sister. In fact, I wanted to be there for her even more, especially as she was carrying a child.

Her next message said, "Please come over." Relief washed over me. It was the invitation I had been waiting and hoping for! Without hesitation, I typed my response and I rushed to get there. I wasn't going to let Olivia change her mind and rescind the invitation!

Within half an hour I was at the front door of our townhouse, well Uncle Mo's townhouse now, I reminded myself. Harrison, the butler, smiled warmly as he opened the door for me, "Ah, Miss Ruth! I am happy to see you and even happier to say that this time, Miss Olivia welcomes your visit. She is waiting in the sitting room. We have tea set up for you both."

"Thank you Harry." I smiled back. "No need to escort me, I can see myself to the sitting room!" I didn't wait for an answer as I rushed to Olivia. I couldn't wait to see her.

As soon as I walked into the room, Olivia stood up and we ran to each other and we hugged.

We also cried together. We cried with happiness as we cherished the fact that we were friends again. We cried with sadness as we regretted that we wasted so much time apart. And I also cried with relief as I felt her small but protruding stomach, she was still pregnant! I didn't even realise it, but I had feared Olivia had done something really stupid and she was no longer pregnant.

Once the tears dried up, we were both ready to talk. "I'm so sorry, Ruth. I was so stupid. I thought that once you were gone, I could get Kane to fall in love with me. Instead he just kept pestering me to convince you to leave Mum. Then I thought that if you came back then he'd realise you'd change, and he wouldn't want you anymore. Then I could swoop in... as I said, I was stupid. He never saw me in that way. Even when I seduced him – it was just the one night, Ruth – but even then, he did it out of pity, or because I was available. He never wanted me. When

I told him we were having a baby, he freaked out! He told me he was too young to be a father and he walked away. That was at New Year's Eve, and so I got drunk, I got high and I blamed you for Kane not wanting our baby and me. In my head, you were the reason for all my unhappiness so you were the last person I wanted to see in the hospital."

It made a lot of sense now. "I get it." I said softly as I held Olivia's hand. It also made sense why Kane came running to me with a very generous offer. He was fuelled by guilt and fear because he knew that any chance we had of getting back together would be ruined once I found out about him and Olivia. He wanted me in his debt, under his control, so there would be no getting away. Not that I ever doubted my decision, but knowing what I knew now, I felt even more vindicated.

"Ruthy, I'm so sorry. Are you sure you're not mad at me?" Olivia asked softly, her face awashed with guilt.

I looked straight into her eyes and answered confidently, "I am a hundred percent sure. I forgive you. I just want to be here for you and my little niece or nephew."

"Thank you! I've been so lonely, you have no idea. I've been so scared and I have no one to turn to. But at first I was mad at you, then I was scared you'd find out and be mad at me anyway so I just kept ignoring you… I'm so glad you're here now." She squeezed my hand tightly and we smiled at each other, just like the way we used to.

A thought suddenly occurred to me, "Can you imagine what Mum would be like as a grandmother…?" We both laughed as we imagined just how much Mum would spoil this baby.

We chatted a little bit more about Mum, my new job and eventually Olivia began quizzing me about my own heartbreak and I shared everything that had happened between Beau and I. Olivia comforted me, got angry on my behalf at Beau for rejecting me, and she coached me that my heart would heal. And I echoed those same words to her.

As we continued to hold each other's hands, I felt at peace. Olivia and I were back to the way we were. We were sisters, once again.

# CHAPTER 21

*I*t was a week before Valentine's Day and love was everywhere I looked. My daily commute to and from work the past week had been pure torture with the reminder of what – rather, who – I was missing in my life. Beau. I missed hanging out with him. I missed having my best friend around. So I did what everyone would do in my situation. I threw myself into work 110%. The best part was that I actually loved my new job. I loved seeing how our practice made such a difference to the lives of our patients. I loved knowing that we were saving lives and giving so many the hope to fight another day. Certainly, when I looked at how far my mum had come from that day when she tried to take her own life, to where she was now – she had new set of friends, she was looking for a job… she was content – I knew that this practice had an important role to play in society. And despite how insignificant my role as a receptionist and assistant may seem, I knew that Dr. Campbell couldn't do what she was doing as well as she was, without someone like me. So I took that responsibility seriously. Already, in the two and half weeks that I had been working there I had implemented a more efficient way to file and started a new contact program for our more 'at risk' clients so that they had someone to talk to everyday. I quickly realised that for some of our clients, their only human contact came only when they walked into the practice. Otherwise, days and even weeks would go by without a conversation. Without support, they were at risk of getting worse and I wanted to do something about it. Dr. Campbell was supportive and appreciated all my ideas.

Within days of starting, I also knew that I would be better at my job if I knew some principles of psychology and so I had devoured every single psychology book available in the practice. The more I read, the more interested I became. So, there I was sitting at the reception desk reading the last of the psychology text books. When I finished the last page, I closed the book and sighed. I wanted to know more. I'd only scratched the surface. I needed to go to the library after work and get more books to read.

Suddenly a thought sparked in my head. What if I went to school to study psychology? And as the idea permeated from my head to my heart, I found myself sitting up with excitement. Yes! This was what I wanted to do. I wanted to be a psychologist! I wanted a practice just like this. I wanted to make a difference just like Dr. Campbell did. It was amazing how your heart and mind sang in unison when you had a full realisation of your life's purpose. Because without any doubt, I knew with all of my heart and all of my mind that life had led me to this exact moment. My future was psychology. I jumped up, wanting to dance, wanting to release the excitement that had grabbed hold of me. I wanted to shout it out. I wanted to call Mum and share the news.

That was until reality hit a second later.

We couldn't afford it. Even with my higher wage, we were barely making ends meet. There was no way we could afford to send me to college. I sat back down, feeling absolutely deflated. Oh well, maybe it wasn't for now. I needed to save up but at least I knew what I wanted to do in the future. I was already farther ahead than I was only a few minutes ago when I had no idea what I wanted to do with my life!

The door suddenly flung open. Dr. Campbell was with our last patient for the day so I was surprised to see a man walk in. Immediately I could tell something was wrong. The man looked to be in his twenties, he was well dressed in a tailored suit but I could tell something wasn't right. "Hi, how can I help you?"

He looked at me for a second then he turned and sat down in one of the couches by the fire.

I stood up and walked closer to the man, "Are you okay?" I asked as I noticed that he wreaked agitation, he was biting his fingernails, his knee was bouncing up and down and his eyes dotted to and fro around the room restlessly.

I'd never seen this man before. I doubted he was a patient and he certainly didn't have an appointment. We didn't normally accept walk-ins but there was certainly something not right with this man. Without saying it, my instinct told me that he was crying out for help.

So I found myself saying, "Thank you for coming to us. Let me get the doctor. Please stay. We can help you."

I was relieved when he acknowledged me with a small nod.

Hurriedly, I knocked at Dr. Campbell's office and when I heard her instruct me to enter, I opened the door and walked in. "I'm so sorry to interrupt, Dr. Campbell, Mrs. Singh. But we have an emergency. A man just walked in and he looks like he needs help."

Dr. Campbell nodded her consent, "Thank you, Ruth. I'll be right out. Please stay with the man, I'll just wrap up with Mrs. Singh." I was just closing the door when I heard Dr. Campbell saying, "Mrs. Singh, I'm so sorry, if you don't mind, I'll need to check this situation-"

Without waiting for Mrs. Singh's answer, I hurriedly made my way to the man waiting at reception. I was relieved to see that he had stayed put. I sat down next to him, frustrated that I didn't know what to say. I wished I knew. I wished I could help him myself.

"Is the doctor coming?" He asked, his breathing was rapid and laboured.

"She is. May I know your name?" He didn't answer.

Finally, less than a minute later, Dr. Campbell's office door opened and both Dr. Campbell and Mrs. Singh walked out.

Dr. Campbell got to work immediately, she quietly spoke to the man and then led him to her office while I organised a next appointment for Mrs. Singh.

An hour later, they still hadn't emerged from the office. There was definitely something wrong if Dr. Campbell was still with the man after a full hour! So while a small part of me was a little nervous that I had broken protocol, I knew that I did the right thing.

It was past 5pm so I started filing, and tidying and packing up for the day. Olivia was coming over for dinner tonight and I had promised to cook, so I was also conscious of wanting to get home as soon as I could while also wanting to stay as long as I could to make sure everything was okay with the man that had walked in.

About fifteen minutes later, the man emerged from the office, immediately followed by Dr. Campbell. "I'll see you in two days, Michael, but please do see your GP first thing tomorrow." Dr. Campbell then turned to me, "Ruth, could you please take down Michael's details and organise time for me to see him on Friday? Thank you." With a smile, she led Michael to my desk where I then proceeded to take Michael's information. I could see that he was a little better. In this business, I already knew that "a little" was already a big task so I was delighted that Dr. Campbell was able to help.

Once Michael was out of sight, I immediately turned to Dr. Campbell to apologise, "I'm sorry Dr. Campbell, I know we don't normally accept walk-ins but I could just tell he needed help."

Dr. Campbell sat at the large wooden desk, her Amazonian features were further exaggerated as I looked up at her while I sat in my office chair. She suddenly smiled, a big smile. In fact you could call it a grin. Yes, Dr. Campbell was grinning at me. "I am proud of you, Ruth. I really am. Not only have you walked in and immediately understood what we are all about, but you have really taken to it like duck to water. I honestly believe you were born for this."

"You think so?" Even as I asked, I already knew the answer. Because I had come to the same conclusion not more than two hours ago. But an affirmation from Dr. Campbell herself was also important to me.

"Absolutely, Ruth. You just saved that man's life. He was walking to the station planning to end it all, but then he saw my office sign and something compelled him to stop by. He was crying out for help without saying it and I am so amazed that you were able to pick up on that."

The full weight of what Dr. Campbell had said hit me like a ton of bricks. I knew the man needed help, but I had no idea just how urgent that cry for help was. If I had turned him away…

More and more, my decision that this was my future, that this was my destiny, became even firmer. Tomorrow, I was going to start saving so I could study psychology. In the meantime, I was going to learn as much as I could here under the amazing tutelage of Dr. Campbell and I would do my part to make as much of a positive impact to our clients as I could.

Dr. Campbell stood up and she picked up the psychology book that I had picked out to take home and re-read. We were going to get out late today and I wasn't going to have enough time to stop by the library so I figured I would re-read the first book I read because I was sure I would have missed something during the first read. This, in particular, was one that Dr. Campbell wrote. "I've noticed you've been reading my psych texts. I'm pretty sure that you would have gone through them all by now."

I nodded in agreement, "Yes I have. They are so interesting. The human mind is a fascinating thing."

"Have you thought about studying psychology and becoming a psychologist yourself? I can see that you have what it takes."

I couldn't believe that we were having this conversation on the same day that I had that same epiphany. "It's so bizarre that you would raise that today of all days, Dr. Campbell. I literally just came to the same conclusion a couple of hours ago. I really do want to be a psychologist. I want to make a difference to people's lives the way that you do. But my dream will have to wait a little bit longer. We can't afford for me to go to school, right no-"

Dr. Campbell didn't let me finish. Instead she dropped the book she was holding on my desk and turned to me with wide eyes and excitement oozing all over her. "I have the perfect solution! You can be my paid intern. I will sponsor your studies and in turn you will work in my practice for the duration of your studies and until you become a qualified psychologist. It's a win-win for both of us. It's perfect!" By now her hands were clasped in front of her, awaiting a response from me.

But my mind was reeling. I couldn't believe such a generous offer would come my way! After so many heartaches and diversions in the past year, I suddenly felt that finally, things were really starting to shift gears. Things were really starting to fall into place!

"You're right, it's perfect. Dr. Campbell, are you really willing to sponsor my studies? You would do that?"

"Yes, absolutely. You will be an incredible psychologist one day, Ruth. I know that without a shadow of a doubt. I will be so proud to be the one to facilitate and guide you into that potential. So, I will do more than just sponsor you and mentor you, I will also make sure you get into the best undergraduate degree. I am a guest lecturer at Oxford and I am sure I can get you a spot there." And with a small laugh, "Ruth, enjoy your freedom now because come September, you're going to be busy!"

I couldn't help myself. I jumped up and hugged Dr. Campbell with as much energy as I could muster. "Thank you, thank you, thank you!"

First, Olivia and I were sisters once again. Now I was about to step into my purpose. There was only one missing piece to really complete the trifecta. But I stopped myself from dwelling on that. No, I must focus on the good things that were happening right now. I wasn't going to wonder where Beau would be right now, what he was doing and definitely would not think about who he was with. I couldn't help it though. Because every time something great happened, Beau was the first person I wanted to share it with. I missed Beau. There was no getting round it.

## CHAPTER 22

# BEAU WARNER

*I* already knew what I was going to see as I walked past the bus stop just outside the soon to be open The Warner Athens Hotel. I also knew what my reaction would be, so I kept my eyes averted as I walked past it and into the renovation site. After nearly a month in Athens, the hotel was now back on schedule. We should be able to open in another month. It had taken some tough decisions to get us back on track, including having to replace the foreman, and it had also required my undivided attention. The latter, I was more than happy to give whole-heartedly because it kept me from wallowing in sorrow and loss. I worked so hard to distract myself and it was working to some degree. That was until last week. Until that advertisement started popping up everywhere - including at the bus stop in front of the hotel. Of all places! Seeing Kane's smug face in the latest Gucci Men campaign was enough to drive me insane. It was a constant reminder of Ruth. Even worse, the thought naturally then led to my imagining Ruth and Kane's happily ever after. Given that it was exactly what I was trying to escape from in the first place, it annoyed me that it would follow me in my sanctuary.

I dropped my brown leather messenger bag on the couch in disgust and plopped myself onto my office chair with a loud sigh. "I'm strong, I'll get through this." I whispered to myself. It was my constant chant but I found that as days went by, the harder it was to forget Ruth. I missed her. There was no denying that.

I wished that I could resent her instead. After all, how could she tell me she loved me one minute and then get herself engaged the next? Not to mention the fact that she really was too young to be engaged! If I didn't see it with my own eyes, I wouldn't have believed it myself. Yet, I did see it. I woke up when I heard the door close behind Ruth that morning. By the time I got to the hallway, she was gone. I followed her to her flat to tell her that I loved her too. And there I became the unwitting witness to Kane's proposal and that kiss. Yes the kiss that would be forever burnt in my head. You couldn't un-see something like that! I certainly didn't want to see more so I dashed out of there as quickly as I could. A part of me regretted that I didn't just tell her how I really felt that night. Maybe if I did, she wouldn't have gotten herself engaged to Kane. But then I remembered how she had cried her heart out to me about Kane that morning in my office. His rejection had really hurt her. It was Kane she truly loved and because I wanted only her happiness, it was the right thing to do to step aside. Besides, I would have regretted taking advantage of a drunk woman. Especially Ruth. Oh it was tempting. She was tempting. When I walked into my bedroom and I saw her on my bed in that red dress, boy I was tempted. And when she told me she loved me, oh how I was tempted! But I loved her too much. Besides, I respected her too much to take advantage of her while in that state. I wanted to prove to her that I loved her for more than her beauty. I took a deep breath as I felt the familiar ache in my heart.

"I'm strong, I'll get through this." Again, I whispered those words to myself. Surely, if I said it enough it would come true?

"Ah, here you are! I came by your flat to take you out to breakfast. Really son, it is far too early to be in the office." Father walked in confidently, carrying a newspaper and his briefcase. He was casually dressed in jeans and a white long-sleeved shirt.

"Father! What are you doing in Athens?" It was good to see him. But I didn't expect him. He didn't give any pre-warning, didn't mention a thing when we were talking yesterday over the phone.

"I'm not checking up on the hotel, if that's what you're thinking." He sat down on one of the chairs facing me and as he did he gently threw the newspaper on the table which then unraveled to reveal that dreaded advertisement.

I couldn't help but whisper, "You're kidding me." That thing was following me everywhere. I quelled my desire to grab the paper and rip it into pieces.

Dad frowned, "What is it?"

"Nothing." I shrugged and looked away.

But my father was a shrewd man. Nothing got passed him. He leaned forward to see what was on the newspaper. "Is it the ad?"

"I love you, you know that, but I really don't want to talk about this, Father. Please." I folded the newspaper and set it aside. "Now, what brings you to Athens?"

"You." He leaned back, linked his hands behind his head and continued, "Your mother has sent me here to check up on you. We have heard that you're doing ridiculous hours. Even more than ever before." Father stood up and walked over to put his hand on my shoulders. "We are worried, son. This is not sustainable. I appreciate all your efforts, I really do, but now that the hotel is back on track, surely it's time to relax a little, huh?"

It was true. I reveled in my exhaustion because it meant that I didn't have the energy to think about Ruth too much, nor have the energy to feel so deeply. The more I felt, the more I worked. But I had to admit that it was all in vain. Nothing worked. Because at the end of each day, when I collapsed in bed, completely depleted, and I closed my eyes to sleep, it was always Ruth I imagined. It was Ruth I dreamed about. Even now, I loved her still. And I missed her so deeply.

Father waited a moment for a response, but when none came, he continued, "I've been where you are. You know that, son. After Naomi left me, I threw myself into my work. But there is one major difference between your situation and what mine was. Naomi left me, but you're the one that left Ruth. Why, I can't fathom."

This really was the last conversation I wanted to have. I didn't want to have to re-live the pain of seeing Ruth kissing Kane. And especially not with my father. So I tried changing the subject. "How's Mother and Steph?"

I was relieved when Father played along. "They are well." He talked about Mother's new charity and then he described Steph's latest boyfriend, a boy from school whose father was a barrister. "Steph's been hanging out in the hotel quite a lot lately because her boyfriend just lives around the corner. Too bad Ruth is no longer there, Steph would have enjoyed spending more time with her."

"No, she'll have to go to Cambridge instead." I knew it was a mistake to take the bait my Father threw, but I couldn't help myself. And I couldn't help the slightly bitter tone that I could detect, even with my own ears.

Father frowned, "What do you mean?"

I shrugged, faking nonchalance, "It's where Kane would have taken her, I'm sure."

"I don't know who this Kane fellow is, but what I do know is that Ruth is in London. She resigned from the hotel to take up a job as a receptionist at a psychologist's practice in London."

The news confused me. No, Father had to be wrong. Why would Ruth have to work? Kane and his family were well off. But what if Father was right? Could that mean that-. I stopped myself. I could not and would not allow myself to hope. "You must be mistaken."

"No son, you are mistaken. I heard it from Nora herself. Ruth is working at that practice run by Naomi's psychologist. What's her name, a Dr…"

"Campbell." I answered.

Father clasped his hands loudly "Yes, that it!"

So Ruth was really working at Dr. Campbell's practice? I couldn't help myself then; hope was ignited and with that my heart started to beat again. "Maybe it didn't work out with Kane after all." I found myself voicing my thoughts, and as I said it I could feel a sliver of joy enter my soul and I allowed myself to think of the possibility that Ruth and I could have a future together. I allowed myself to dream.

Father shrugged, "I don't know, son. But even if she is with this boy, isn't she worth fighting for?"

Yes, Ruth was worth fighting for. Ruth and I were so good together. I loved the fact that we were great friends, that we always had a good laugh, that we always seemed to understand each other. Memories flooded of those little moments we spent together – ice skating, the renovations, New Year's Eve ball, all those memories were stitched together and they played in my head and activated my resolve.

But why was Father supportive all of a sudden? "I got the sense, Father, that there was a time you didn't think Ruth was worth me fighting for."

"Ah yes, you would be correct there, son. But since then Nora, your mother and Steph have been in my ear telling me how amazing Ruth is. How good she is for you. Everything I've heard about her goes against everything I would have expected from a selfish and greedy young woman I had painted her to be in my mind. I knew then that it was my own prejudice that coloured my view. So, I've changed my mind. I acted like a fool at the Ball. If you love her, son, and it's obvious you do, go and fight for her."

No, I was the fool. Why didn't I stay and fight for her love? Why didn't I try to convince her that I was a better match for her? I should have told her how I felt and let her decide who she wanted to be with. I had allowed pride and hurt to win and as a consequence allowed Kane free reign. I practically opened the door and allowed Kane in when I should have been guarding the door with my dear life. He wasn't good enough for her. He couldn't make her happy the way I could. He wouldn't and couldn't love her the way I would and did. I just needed to convince Ruth of that. I was up for the task, even if it took forever.

With renewed gusto, I stood up quickly and grabbed my bag, "Father, let's go. We have a plane to catch."

# CHAPTER 23

*M*um and I were cozied up on the couch with a glass of wine and a box of chocolate. It was Valentine's night and we were watching the re-run of the BBC adaptation of Pride and Prejudice. It was the Colin Firth version – our favourite version – so we were having a lot of fun as we recited their lines, a true testament of how often we had watched the series. The fact that we had this in common was a happy surprise. We actually had never watched it together and we found ourselves wondering how we never knew just how much we had in common.

We were up to the second episode when a loud banging at our door interrupted us. "I'll get it." I said to Mum, then louder, "Coming!" I shouted as I jumped out of the couch and within seconds I opened the door to see a very frantic-looking Nora.

"Oh good, you're in!" Nora gave me a quick hug and then with quick breaths she continued, "I'm so sorry to interrupt your evening, Ruth, but I am desperate and I need your help!"

Nora was the best friend any one could have. She had been a great support to me and my mum, so without hesitation I replied, "Of course, Nora. Anything. What can I do for you?"

"Tonight is the Valentines Gala at the hotel. It's our biggest event! We raise funds for the British Heart Foundation and the whole town goes to this thing - even the royals make an appearance! But there's a stomach virus passing through the restaurant staff who would have been working at tonight's Gala. We've called caterers but we are still down five staff. I've been able to cover three with our housekeeping team but-"

"Of course I'll help!" It was the least I could do.

"Yes absolutely, Ruth will help and so will I, if there is anything I can do?" Mum was also at the door by now and she gave Nora a fond hug.

"'Many hands make light work' or whatever that saying – so yes! Thank you, thank you! We need to head over to the hotel now. Is that okay with you two?"

We were both in our pyjamas. "Meet you out by the stairs in five minutes." I said quickly as we jumped into action.

I got dressed in jeans and a sweater and quickly tied my hair in a tight bun. I looked forward to stepping into The Warner again and hopefully see many familiar faces. The one face I did miss, I knew I wouldn't see. He was all the way in Athens and probably on a date with a gorgeous eligible Greek bachelorette. I felt the familiar pinch in my heart and I tried to ignore it, as I brushed my teeth, grabbed my bag and jacket and headed out.

Two hours later, I was dressed in a crisp white shirt, black tie, black pants and serving a tray of wagyu beef canapé. The ballroom was elegantly decorated in red and gold accents and centre stage was a famous UK band playing classic love songs. Nora was right, the entire town seemed to be at this event, including Eve, her dad and stepmother who were being very nice as they took a piece of the canapé I offered them. Amazingly, even as I served former friends and acquaintances, I felt no shame. Instead I was confident as I greeted and chatted with the guests. I had come to a point in my life where I not only accepted my situation, but I was happy with where life was taking me. Finally, I knew that I had something special to offer this world. That I could make a real difference.

"I do miss hanging out with you, Ruth. We used to have so much fun!" Eve cooed then she daintily consumed the tiny morsel of beef.

I smiled warmly at Eve in response. There really were no hard feelings on my part. "I miss you too Eve. Let me know when you're free and we can do something." And with another warm smile, "I better go and keep serving these canapés."

I turned around and I found myself in front of Steph and Beau's parents. Steph was the first to say something, "Ruth!" She gave a cheek-to-cheek kiss. "So good to see you!"

"Good to see you too Steph." And with a polite smile I turned to the elegant couple standing in front of me, "Good evening to you Mr. and Mrs. Warner."

I expected a cold reception from Mr. Warner but instead he returned my smile and nodded an acknowledgement. Mrs Warner directed a large smile my way and winked. I didn't have time to contemplate the sudden change in attitude especially from Mr. Warner as another guest dropped by to greet their hosts.

I was serving the final pieces of beef on my tray when I vaguely heard the band's front man make an announcement. I wasn't paying attention to it though as I continued to chat to the couple I was serving who knew Uncle Mo and in fact attended the funeral for Dad and the boys. So it wasn't until I heard Beau's voice on the microphone that my ears pricked up and I turned around to see him standing on stage holding an acoustic guitar. "Good evening! Thank you all for coming tonight." I nearly dropped my tray. I had multiple emotions at that exact moment – surprise (what was he doing here? And what was he doing with a guitar?), joy (it was so good to see him!); anticipation (I hoped that I would get to talk to him!); sadness (but he didn't want me, in fact he left me without even acknowledging that I had confessed my love to him); love (yes, I still loved him. I felt it even as I watched him adjust the microphone on its stand).

By now, the crowd had stopped talking and all eyes were on him. And I couldn't take mine off his gorgeous face.

"Those of you who know me would know I normally don't play in public. In fact I have only ever played this instrument in my room!" The audience responded with a laugh. "But tonight I wanted to show someone just how special she is to me-" My heart felt like it was about to explode. Surely he couldn't be referring to me? How would he have even known that I was in the audience? No, he must have brought back someone he met in Athens. I turned to leave, knowing I wouldn't be able to survive the heartbreak of seeing him declaring his love to someone else. I turned around and took two steps, "-and I wanted to show the whole world that I would do anything, even play in public, to have her in my life. Ruth, I am in love with you. I wrote this song for you." I stopped walking as the full force of emotions hit me. Beau was declaring his love for me!

I pivoted back around to look at him and saw that this time his eyes had found me in the crowd. Our eyes met as he strummed the first strain of melody. And when he started singing, "When I gave you up, I didn't really know; just what I was giving up, oh why did I let you go...", our eyes remained connected and I knew what happiness really felt like.

Beau continued to sing, his gaze never left my face and it was like there was no one else in the room. He was singing this song only for me. We loved each other. Nothing else mattered at that moment. Doubts, questions, insecurities, they all fell to the wayside. There was only this. Only us.

When the song was coming to its end, Beau walked away from the microphone so I could only hear the subtle strumming of the guitar and his voice seemed like a whisper, until the crowd parted and he was right in front of me as he sang, "So please tell me how you love me so; And I'll hold on to you always, never let you go; We're meant to be together; Oh now and forever; let's dance to this music together; Oh now and forever..."

As the last strains of his voice drifted off, the crowd cheered enthusiastically. I was smiling, most likely a goofy smile as our eyes continued to speak the unspoken words of love. Someone in the crowd collected his guitar and my tray and we were both empty-handed as we stood facing each other. We had an audience, but we didn't care.

"You can write music, sing and play the guitar. Are there any more secrets you've been hiding from me?" I teased as I allowed my gaze to take in just how handsome Beau was, especially dressed in his tuxedo.

"Only that I am completely and utterly in love and devoted to you, Ruth. The moment I opened my office closet and saw you hiding in there," we both laughed as he said that, "and when I held your hand to help you up, I didn't want to ever let you go. And I still don't, Ruth. Tonight is a set up. We didn't need your help tonight. It's a ruse to get you here because I want to demonstrate just how much I care for you and love you. I don't know whether you're with Kane or not-"

I was surprised when he mentioned Kane. "I'm not with Kane." I clarified as I stepped closer, "Why would I be with Kane, when I'm in love with you?"

"You're not with Kane?" He asked and I responded with a shake of my head. "So it really is true, you didn't quit to go with him to Cambridge?"

I shook my head again as an answer. "You're not engaged?" I shook my head yet again and showed him my empty left ring finger as proof. His smile widened then he shook his head as he placed his right hand on his forehead, "I'm an idiot. We were in love with each other this whole time..."

This time, I nodded in response then asked, "So what are we going to do about it?"

Without hesitation, he answered, "This." He took my hand and pulled me into his arms. Then his lips touched mine.

In the background, the crowd cheered. It was Valentines after all, so who wouldn't appreciate a love story unfolding before their very eyes? And when the band struck up another love song, couples started to dance around us, spurred on by the romance they had just witnessed.

Beau and I were oblivious to all this. Our attention was only for each other.

"You realise, now that I know you can sing and play that I'm going to get you to sing and play for me all the time?" I teased as I placed my hands around his neck.

"I will happily sing and play for you for the rest of our lives, Ruth." It was a promise, and one he sealed with a kiss. And as the music faded in the background, I melted in Beau's arms, and all I could feel and all I could think of was the kiss. After all, our kiss felt like its own love song, and the music was even sweeter than I could have ever imagined.

# SEVEN YEARS LATER

"Ruth, where are you?" Mum sounded worried over the phone. "Don't worry Mum. I'll be there soon." I promised as I rushed to pack up my books and the papers scattered around Dr. Campbell's office. I had a paper I needed to submit before we went away so I decided to escape the ruckus and madness that had taken over the flat in the last couple of days and find peace and tranquility right here. But I knew I couldn't escape for too long. Sooner or later, Mum would come calling and sure enough, she did.

Once I was packed, I got back on my laptop, quickly uploaded my paper onto the online gateway and with utter relief, I hit the 'submit' button. There, now I didn't have to worry about that and I could just focus on today.

I was now a qualified psychologist and in two years I would become a qualified clinical psychologist. I was enjoying my Ph.D and was passionate about my dissertation on ongoing patient care. It was a lot of study and a lot of research and papers and practical work but I loved every minute of it. I especially loved having my own patients to work with. Dr. Campbell's practice had grown as we shared the workload between us. It had grown so much that we even had a practice manager as well a receptionist.

My phone buzzed again, "Where are you?" It was a message from Olivia.

This was followed immediately by another message, this time it was Nora, "Your Mum is starting to panic. Please come home."

It was definitely time to head back home. I flipped close by laptop and ran out of the building.

As soon as I walked into the flat, I was swept into a tidal wave of activity. Two hours later, dressed in ivory lace, I stared at my reflection in the mirror as I noted every detail of my gown, veil, hair, make up. Everything was exactly how I pictured it. I couldn't wait to see Beau's reaction. I couldn't wait to see Beau. I couldn't wait to start our married lives together.

"You're beautiful, Auntie Ruth!" A small voice gushed behind me and I turned to see my niece, Bella, standing behind me dressed in her white dress and a garland made of white posies around her temples. Bella was a mirror image of Olivia at that age.

"Thank you, gorgeous Bella. You look beautiful yourself." I bent down to give her a hug.

Mum walked into my room in a rush, "Time to go, the car has arri-" She suddenly stopped when she saw me. "Oh Ruth, you look beautiful! Your Dad…" She sat down on the bed as tears streamed from her eyes.

I knew how Mum felt. I was happy, in fact there were moments I felt that I was too happy! Yet despite that, we also knew we were missing three special people that should have been here with us today. Especially Dad, he would have proudly walked me down the aisle. I wiped a stray tear and I hugged Mum as tight as I could. "I miss him too, Mum. I miss Kyle and Mark."

Mum wiped her tears with her handkerchief and she smiled. "Especially on days like today. Speaking of, come on, we have to go. We still have a long drive ahead of us." Mum got up, checked her make up in the mirror and rushed out of the room with the same energy she had coming in. I was so proud of Mum. She had developed her confidence and inner strength in the past seven years and she now worked as a sales consultant at friend's boutique.

Checking myself in the mirror one last time, I took a deep breath and followed Mum out of the room.

The wedding was to take place in the grounds of Beau's parents' estate, Rose Hall. They had wanted us to stay and prepare in the Hall or even at a local Inn however I had insisted that I wanted to be home. From tonight onwards, the flat wouldn't be home any more so I wanted one last night there. It well and truly had become home. Between Mum and I, we earned enough income to have moved to a bigger place, but we both decided against it. Despite the rough start, that flat now held very fond memories.

"Are you nervous?" Olivia teased, as she sat at the front passenger seat of the white Rolls Royce. She was my Maid of Honour and Olivia had worked tirelessly in preparation for the wedding. Her creative mind had been invaluable in styling the wedding and I was more than happy to allow her free reign. After all, who wouldn't allow "UK's most exciting fine arts genius" (as quoted by a leading art critic during Olivia's latest showing) to style their wedding?

I shook my head, "Not at all. I'm excited." That was the truth. The last seven years with Beau was a lot of fun. Oh it wasn't perfect but there was no doubting that we loved each other and that we were soul mates. I was marrying my best friend. From the very beginning of our relationship, we knew we were heading down the aisle together. We just didn't know when, given we were still quite young and I had my studies.

Yet if Beau had his way, we would have been married by now. I knew he was more than eager to call me his wife, eager for us to live together and start a family together. But Beau would always put his wishes second to mine. I wanted to finish my masters first and so he waited patiently.

Hence it wasn't a complete surprise that when that day finally came, he didn't wait a moment longer. He arranged a private celebratory dinner on the night of my graduation ceremony on the rooftop of his flat, complete with a thousand candles, a cellist and Chef Leon cooking up a seven-course degustation meal.

"You've really outdone yourself, Beau. This is amazing. Thank you." I said gratefully as I finished the last spoonful of salted caramel parfait.

Beau stood up and then he knelt down in front of me. When I looked around, we were alone. The cellist, the servers, Chef Leon, they had exited stage left.

"Ruth, when I first declared my love for you, I did it in public. The whole world was there. This time, I will be asking you the most important question I'm ever going to ask and I want it to just be you and I."

I knew what he was going to ask. My heart felt like it was going to beat out of my chest in pure excitement and joy. My mind was already screaming 'Yes!' and he hadn't even asked yet.

Beau took my hands and his eyes continued to pierce into mine, "Ruth, the last six years has only made me fall deeper and deeper in love with you. We are partners in every sense of the word. I have no doubt that we belong together. Ruth Rosalind Triggs, please say you'll be my wife. Let's do forever." He took out a velvet box out of his back pocket and opened it to reveal a sparkling cushion cut diamond ring with a diamond-studded band. It was large and it was beautiful. But it wasn't the ring that impressed me; it was the man offering it to me.

"Yes to forever." I whispered.

Fast-forwarded a year later and the big day had arrived, a few minutes later our car was finally at Rose Hall and within a few seconds, Mum was walking me down the beautiful garden and towards the large rose covered arch where Beau was waiting. He looked so handsome. And he was mine forever.

The orchestra started to play as we approached the aisle and Beau turned to look for me. His smile deepened when he spotted me, then I saw him take a deep breath and then wiped his eyes. Colin stood next to him and he must have said something to tease Beau because Beau laughed even as he kept his eyes firmly on me.

Finally, I was face to face with Beau. "You look beautiful." He whispered. "Even more beautiful than usual and I didn't think that could be possible."

"You look beautiful yourself." I said as I wiped an imaginary dust off his chest.

"Why, thank you." His voice was a mere whisper so that our conversation was for our ears alone. Then he stepped closer and whispered into my ear, "I'm so glad that you happened to hide in my closet. Imagine if you had accidently hidden in Paul Callahan's closet." He teased. Paul was the Reception Manager. We both looked at Paul, seated on the third row with his wife of thirty years. He looked embarrassed; he was probably wondering why the bride and groom were looking at him.

I laughed and whispered back, "Yes, imagine, I could be marrying him instead of you."

The bishop, a friend of the Warners, cleared his throat, wanting to get our attention. "Shall we proceed?" he said in good humour.

"Yes, by all means, please do. I am eager to start our forever." I declared whole-heartedly and our friends and family cheered in celebration.

I couldn't help it. I laughed.

My laughter was a genuine outward manifestation of the happiness I felt inside. I was truly happy.

As we said our vows, my happiness deepened because I knew we both meant every single word we uttered.

As Beau bent down to kiss me after the bishop declared us Husband and Wife, I knew that life had led me to this exact moment.

And as we danced in the ballroom later that evening with the music blaring in the background, I also knew this was exactly where I wanted to be. I was dancing in the arms of the man that was meant to be my dance partner. Forever.

### THE END

# A NOTE FROM THE AUTHOR

The Heart of Ruth is a modern retelling of the Book of Ruth in the Bible. I have always loved Biblical stories with strong female characters and have often imagined them in today's world.

Ruth is a favourite of mine. What I love about Ruth is that she followed her heart and she followed what she knew was the right thing even though it was going to lead to a harder path. Importantly, I love that her decision to stay with Naomi - her loyalty - eventually leads her to Boaz, who was able to give them an abundant life and secure their legacy. This really is a story of hope.

If you're going through your own pain or loss, if you're going through a storm, if things are hard, just know that it won't last forever. It'll only be for a season. Just take the next right step, one at a time, and eventually you'll see that you'll be laughing again. And know that there is one who said that He will never leave you, He is there with you to help and comfort you, all you have to do is call out His name, "Jesus".

www.ingramcontent.com/pod-product-compliance
Lightning Source LLC
Chambersburg PA
CBHW020616250626
47154CB00004B/1536